REALM OF FORGOTTEN DREAMS

REALM OF FORGOTTEN DREAMS

2024 FICTION FANTASTIC
YOUNG WRITERS
SHORT FICTION CONTEST

Wordcrafters in Eugene

Our Mission

We believe in the power of story. Stories tell us who we are, and who we can be. Wordcrafters empowers writers and readers by increasing access to community, craft, and inspiration. We provide a home for sharing knowledge and stories with each other and future generations to cultivate a more empathetic, creative, and courageous world.

Our Vision

At Wordcrafters, we believe in the power of storytelling and its ability to create community. Wordcrafters works to expand access to who gets to call themselves a writer, to disrupt the gatekeeping around storytelling, and advocate for and celebrate vibrantly diverse voices, especially those that have been marginalized and excluded. We believe channeling the power of our creative voices creates braver, more empathetic, and more equitable places to live.

(+ all the chocolate your writer-heart needs)

Wordcrafters in Eugene

Staff

Daryll Lynne Evans, Executive Director

Jorah LaFleur, WITS Coordinator & Teaching Artist

Jeaux Bartlett, Giving & Connection Catalyst

Leah Velez, Programming Manager

Audrey Quinn, Marketing Wordsmith

Emmanuelle Furhiman, Intern

Board of Directors

Matthew Lowes, President

Miriam Gershow, Secretary

Christina Lay, Treasurer

Rosemary Nigro

Carla Orcutt

Phosphor Emery Alethes

Anthology Staff

Daryll Lynne Evans, Jeaux Bartlett,
Audrey Quinn

Individual Donors & Members

Justin Ahrenholtz
Deniss Albers
Phosphor Emery Alethes
Laura Allen
Gerri Almand
Ella Amos Killingsworth
Jennifer Anderson
Nanci Axelton
Mark Barbour
Marsha Barr
Jeaux Bartlett
Jubilee Barton-Ganem
Mark Beardsley
Katie Bernstein
Amanda Bird
Korrin Bishop
John Blyler
Judith Boice
Rose Brant
Ivy Broiles
Valerie Brooks
Elizabeth Bruno
Kendall Cable
Bill Cameron
Dawn Capone
Phil Carson
Denise-Christine
Diane Choplin
Nina Chordas
Simone Cooper
Liane Cordes

Chad Crabtree
Carol Dennis
Melissa Denny
Edi dePencier
Mary Durfee
Elizabeth Dykstra
Kelly Eastlund
Stephanie Edwards
Vicki Elmer
Daryll Lynne Evans
Rebecca Fay
Barbara Forrest-Ball
Carol Frischmann
Manny Frishberg
Miriam Gershow
Carole Gibson
Amalia Gladhart
Henry Goswick
Bobbi Grace
Lynda Green
Hester Grove
Annika Hanson
Bryan Haynes
Allegra Helfenstein
Kirstin Hierholzer
Carolyn Holihan
Cheryl Holland
Johnathan Howe
Marilyn Hull
Kim Hunter
Polly Jackson

Denise Jessup
Laura Keys
Linda Klein
Leonore Lakshmanan
Alexis Lanham
Cori Larson
Peggy Laurance
Christina Lay
Ben Lilley
Cindy Lipton
Elizabeth Lyon
Dana Magliari
Annette Marcus
Amy Marsh
Eliza Master
Stan Matthews
Rebecca McCroskey
Joshua Mertz
Diana Nadeau
Darlene Neale
Rosemary Nigro
Nina Nolen
Melanie Oommen
Carla Orcutt
Cheryl Owen-Wilson
Shiela Pardee
Sue Parman
Tai Passaretti
Paul Pastrone
Nancy-Lou Polk
Stephanie Pressman
Emily Pyle
Aubrey Raney-Avers
Laurie Reed
Hazel Robin
Ken Robinson
Megan Rose

Patricia Ruane
Susan Sabia
Jill Sager
Connor Salisbury
Gale Ann Salvador
Ellen Saunders
Joachim Schulz
Sarah Scott
Althea Seloover
Marianne Senhouse
Inga Silva
Kaya Singer
Roni Slye
Lanie Smith
Jeany Van Meltebeke
Snider
David Solbach
Barb Stevens-Newcomb
Shanna Swezey
Carol Taylor
Wendy Thelander
Carrie Thomas
Kathy Thomas
Barbara Tobin
Rosalind Trotter
Annie Tupek
Rebecca Tursa
Jodi Wainwright
Ann Walker
Kathleen Walker
Larina Warnock
Jennifer Weaver
Aldis Weible
Nancy West
Joseph Whitson
Eric Witchey
Pearl Wolfe

Sponsors

Elizabeth George Foundation

Harvest Foundation

James F. and Marion L. Miller Foundation

Luminare Press

MillsDavis Foundation

Oregon Arts Commission

Contents

On Winged Dreams

Sweet Dreams Are Made of This

INTRODUCTION

"Come and trip it as ye go, On the light fantastick toe."

—*John Milton, L'Allegro*

Welcome to the Realm of Forgotten Dreams. Here, you will trip the light fantastic chasing those hazy dream-fragments that follow you, inspire you, and sometimes haunt you in the waking world. In the stories that follow, these young writers have dared to dream up worlds futuristic and fantastical, characters comical and complicated, exploits thrilling and outlandish, and tales tragic and triumphant that will leave you laughing, crying, thinking, and—most importantly—*dreaming* anything is possible.

Fiction Fantastic remains one of the few opportunities in Lane County to showcase student writing or provide creative writing instruction. In our eleventh year of the contest in 2024, 100 entries poured in from across Lane County, young writers took part in creative writing workshops, teachers loved the engaging curriculum (and stickers!) we developed to help bring creative writing to their classrooms, and—thanks to Luminare Press—young writers get to see their words in print in the Winners Anthology!

The selection process is highly competitive for Fiction Fantastic. First, stories go through rounds of blind judging, read by a panel of twenty volunteer judges made up of writers, educators, and community members. Then the top stories in each grade grouping go to our celebrity judge (still without identifying student info), who selects the winning stories and placements. Finalists learn their placement at the Fiction Fantastic awards ceremony, where they also get to share a short reading from their work.

We cannot do this work without the tremendous support of our community of writers, educators, volunteers, and parents, not to mention the foundations, local businesses, and donors like you who support our youth programs.

Fiction Fantastic is a part of our Writers in the Schools programs for young writers. Wordcrafters in Eugene has built a strong foundation for our Writers in the Schools (WITS) program. Since its launch, the WITS program has served over 7,800 students across Lane County, including schools in rural and under-served areas. WITS Programs include a monthly Write Club, creative writing summer camps, and more.

This anthology illustrates the power of imagination and the importance of story, particularly in trying times. Join us as we continue to nurture our young writers and future storytellers so that they, in turn, can dream up the stories of resilience, hope, and fortitude we need to face the challenges life presents us. Read on!

Sincerely,

Daryll Lynne Evans, Executive Director,
Wordcrafters in Eugene

About Fiction Fantastic
Judge Sander Moffitt

Sander Moffitt is a recent graduate of Brown University, with a degree in Biology and English. Her writing experience ranges from science communication on endangered plants to fantasy novels about necromancers and bones. Sander's Wordcrafters claim to fame is that she was a three consecutive year Fiction Fantastic winner in high school. Outside of writing, Sander enjoys drawing, exploring, and tending to a small army of houseplants.

2024 Fiction Fantastic Winners

K-2 Spotlight

"The Falcon's Egg" by Roya Talebreza-May,
Ridgeline Montessori Public Charter School

Elementary School

1st Place: "The Strength of the Weak" by Sidney Johnson,
Pleasant Hill Elementary School

2nd Place: "Zonglou" by Leo Kuhl,
Charlemagne French Immersion Elementary School

3rd Place: "Stranded" by Kane Lowell,
Creslane Elementary School

Honorable Mention: "Secret Recipe" by Jocelyne
Stevenson, Pleasant Hill Elementary School

Middle School

1st Place: "A Murder of Crows" by Keiko Sophie Weible,
Spencer Butte Middle School

2nd Place: "The Green Ember" by Kai Suzumura,
Ridgeline Montessori Public Charter School

3rd Place: "Let Go" by Nina Kuhl,
Roosevelt Middle School

Honorable Mention: "Shipwrecked in the Sky"
by Hunter Lowell, Creswell Middle School

High School

1st Place: "The Rose Theater" by Ishika Chakraborty, South Eugene High School

2nd Place: "Orbit" by JT Myers, Elmira High School

3rd Place: "Whispers in the Woods" by Lauren Ellison, Marist High School

Honorable Mention: "Gold Dust Books" by L. Stepp, Creswell High School

Honorable Mention: "To the Ends of the Earth" by Brianna R. Bird, Springfield High School

Editor's Note

"[I]f you can learn a simple trick, Scout, you'll get along a lot better with all kinds of folks. You never really understand a person until you consider things from his point of view [...] until you climb into his skin and walk around in it."

—Atticus Finch in To Kill a Mockingbird by Harper Lee

Fair warning, Dear Reader.

The stories you're about to read are those of young writers finding their voice and telling their stories. At Wordcrafters, we are firm believers in giving young writers the space to share their stories and learn that their voices matter. While we edit for clarity and style, we do not censor student work. In these stories, the authors poke, prod, and push boundaries; conduct thought experiments and explorations of style and genre; and try on other perspectives and ways of being in the world. There are definitely a few swear words, some challenging themes and material, and occasionally a few stumbles as these authors work out the many nuances of, as Atticus Finch puts it, "climb[ing] into [another's] skin and walk[ing] around in it"—exactly what we hope for from these curious, inventive writers engaging with their world!

On Winged Dreams

A Murder of Crows

by Keiko Sophie Weible

Spencer Butte Middle School

Jason Lupus was terrible at being a noble. Well, that's what everyone said anyway. So what if he burned half the estate library at age three and made the simple mistake of slipping a psychedelic mushroom into a stew at age five?

His parents, Augustus and Atlanta Lupus, were afraid that he would destroy the land that they had made so many shady dealings with so many strange people to acquire. They strove to get their younger son out of the public eye as soon as possible.

One day when Jason was six, a group of renegades stormed into the family estate. Jason, left entirely alone at the time, sensed danger when he discovered that none of the countless priceless objects were being stolen.

Scared, he escaped the house by climbing down the tree next to his window and hiding in a mud puddle. When his family returned, they thought he had been kidnapped, and were ecstatic.

Until Jason came back.

Noticing that they could turn the situation around, his parents crafted the perfect excuse to get rid of him. They told him that people wanted to hurt him, and to keep him safe, he would have to work as a servant until he could protect himself.

Ten years later

Evening quickly faded into night as Jason put out the lamps in the library, being very careful about it, when a tendril of smoke wafted into the room. At first, he thought it was a lamp that had stuttered out, but other than the servants candles, all lights had already been extinguished. Curious, he went to investigate.

The trail was thin but traceable, and Jason knew the halls well. As he passed the kitchen, he (quite literally) ran into his best friend, Kain Hailer. The two boys ended up in a loose jumble on the floor.

"Sorry, Kain," he grunted.

"You're good," Kain grunted back. "C'mon. It's late and I'm tired."

Forgetting about the smoke, Jason got up and walked to the servants' quarters with his friend as they compared how the day had been. It might have been the only thing that saved him from what happened next. Halfway across the courtyard, the estate exploded.

* * *

A loud ringing brought Jason back to consciousness. He opened his eyes to see his home and life blown to bits and scattered around him. Fire was everywhere. Kain was nowhere to be seen. Despair settled into Jason's heart as he stared at the flames.

Realizing there was nothing left for him, he stood up and left the ruins.

After hours of walking, he saw a small inn at the side of the road. For lack of a better plan, he went inside.

The inn was named the Wanderer's Rest and it certainly was cozy. There was a woman, maybe thirty years old, sitting behind the check-in counter. She looked up and smiled.

"Are you looking for a place to stay?" she asked gently. "You look like you need one."

Jason just nodded, relieved that she hadn't asked about anything else. The woman handed over a room key and directed him to an open table off the lobby.

"I should pay you," he said, voice grating like metal on metal.

"Think nothing of it. Your food will be out shortly," she said, smiling again.

There weren't many people staying at the inn that night. A few older men sat at the bar playing a high-stakes game of poker. A group of kids were laughing in the corner. One patron stood out to Jason, a girl around his age with storm-gray eyes and jet-black hair with streaks of gold and silver. Shivering, Jason turned away. Something about her reminded him of Kain, and thinking about Kain . . . well, thinking about Kain made him want to scream until his voice was hoarser than it already was because the world had left him without a friend, family, or anything at all.

A voice startled him out of his thoughts and he realized that his eyes were full of tears.

"Here's your food," the innkeeper said. "I hope you enjoy it. Put the dishes in the sink over there when you're done, OK?"

Nodding, he looked at the food. A bowl of soup, a couple of warm buttered rolls, and a fresh apple. After eating, he put his dishes in the sink and dragged himself up a flight of stairs to his room. Crashing onto the bed, sleep overcame him. With it came strange dreams.

Just a few hours later, a noise woke Jason up. It was the raspy *haw-caw* of a raven, but the sun had only just started to cast its glow on the world.

"Why is that bird awake?!" he thought groggily.

Just as he was trying to fall back to sleep, another sound came. The creak of a floorboard. He tightened his hands into fists under the sheets. *Creak, creak, creak.* There had been a creaky board on the landing right in front of his room.

Had he left his key in the lock? Suddenly, there was a loud crash, followed by a yell, and then silence.

Slowly, Jason got up, opened the door a crack, and peeked through, sure that someone was going to jump him. Instead, the girl he had seen in the lobby was outside, calmly dragging the limp forms of four black-clothed men into a loose jumble on the landing, tying them together with a length of slightly frayed rope. She looked much the same as the night before except she now had a pack slung across her shoulders, and her distinctive tri-colored hair was pulled back in a tight bun.

After a moment, she looked up.

"Well, don't just stand there, we need to go," she said.

When Jason failed to respond, for he was quite sure he was still dreaming, she simply grabbed his arm and dragged him down the stairs. Despite looking like she could barely lift a potted plant, this girl was quite strong. It took getting dragged down the stairs and almost out the door for him to even consider objecting.

"Who are you?" he finally asked.

"Morrigan," she said. "No more questions. Not now. In case you didn't understand, Jason Lupus, you are no longer safe from the cult."

Now Jason was thoroughly confused. Why was he being attacked? Who exactly was Morrigan? What cult? What disturbed him most was that Morrigan and the people of this cult knew and cared that he was alive.

* * *

MORRIGAN LED JASON WEST INTO ALL SPIRITS FOREST, A place where anyone with a shred of common sense wouldn't dare go. Jason remembered stories told to him as a child about the place. How, out of the few people who dared to enter, even fewer survived and those who did came back, delirious and confused, saying that a race of people who turned into crows lived in the heart of the forest. Morrigan marched right in without breaking stride.

As the sun began to set, Morrigan finally slowed and stopped them for the night. From her pack she produced food and blankets. The food was basic: some bread, meat, and cheese, enough for a small meal.

Finally, she looked up and said, "Get some wood for a fire."

Jason was confused.

"If someone's after me, isn't it better not to?"

"Trust me, we're more vulnerable without it."

Unnerved, Jason did as he was told. As he gathered wood a little way away from the camp, a beast emerged from some bushes to his left. The massive creature looked like a cat, with a lean muscular body, huge bared teeth, and a barbed tail. It also had glowing amber eyes, intelligent eyes. The eyes of a killer.

"Come to me," the eyes seemed to say. "You are nothing, you are broken. You have nothing to live for. I can end your suffering."

Jason froze in place, unable to move. The beast tensed, knowing that its prey was giving up. Just as it was about to spring, Morrigan hurtled out of the trees, yelling and waving a branch over her head.

The beast pounced, but Jason had unfrozen and was able to dive out of the way. The creature turned and fled into the forest.

Morrigan looked down at Jason and said, "That, right there, is why we need a fire."

* * *

As the days wore on, the two travelers slowly became friends. Morrigan no longer treated Jason as baggage and slowed down in her frantic dash toward the center of the forest. Morrigan, Jason discovered, had an amazing sense of humor.

On the evening of the fifth day, Jason finally asked the questions that had been burning in the back of his mind. At first, he asked simple questions like, where she was from, if she had any family, stuff like that. Morrigan answered all the questions seriously but vaguely. They talked as the sun began to set, the fading light struggling to break through the canopy. As the first stars began to appear through the trees, Jason asked his final question.

"Where are you taking me?" he asked, lying back on his blanket as his eyelids began to droop.

Morrigan smiled sadly, staring into the coals, the only remnants of the fire that they had made a few hours before. Then she looked up, staring into the distance.

"Somewhere I wish I didn't need to," she said, but Jason barely heard. He was already falling asleep.

* * *

In the middle of the night, two men stalked through the forest, silent and forbidding as death itself. Their names were Corvus and Rawkh. Corvus was stocky in build and

          Winners Anthology

looked like the type whose brain was roughly the size of a walnut. Rawkh on the other hand was tall and lean, his build that of a predator. Despite all appearances, both men were wickedly smart and skilled hunters.

The two came to the encampment. Smoldering coals were the only remnants of the fire. They had found their prey.

Corvus grinned down at the two figures. "Look, Rawkh," he said. "Looks like Morrigan found herself a friend."

"Too bad he won't survive," Rawkh said with a cackle.

"You should take care not to wake your quarry," Morrigan said. She was the figure on the right. Rolling up onto all fours, she stared unblinkingly at the two men. "And if memory serves, Corvus, your son was this doomed boy's friend."

Corvus gritted his teeth and pushed past Morrigan. He grabbed one side of Jason's blanket.

"Come on, Rawkh, I can't do this by myself," he said.

Rawkh walked over and stood across from the other man, with the boy between them. Then, through some arcane magic, the two men began to transform. The changes came rapidly. Arms became wings, clothes became feathers, mouths and noses fused into beaks. Where there had been men mere moments before, there were now giant crows. Each grabbed two corners of the blanket and took off.

As they flew away into the night, the single raspy caw of a raven followed. It sounded almost like an apology.

As the night wore on, Jason was flown over miles of forest. The leaves of oak and maple trees flashed dimly past, mixed with the coarse needles of pine and cedar. Somehow, none of it woke him up.

The moon was reaching the apex of its nightly journey as the two crows banked toward a clearing at the heart of the forest. At first the opening between the trees looked unremarkable, but looking again, things got strange. The shadows were too dark and the leaves in the trees were accented a bit too much. It was like looking at a normal scene through warped glass.

As the two shapeshifters and their human cargo neared the clearing, they, too, began to look warped. Then there was a flash of light, and the three beings were gone to a place that no human could see.

* * *

Jason woke up in a cell. At first, he was delirious and confused. Where was he, and where was Morrigan?

Then he remembered that she had said that a cult was hunting him. Could it be that they had found him and had captured him? If that was the case, had they hurt her? Did she need help?

Jason panicked until he heard the faraway sound of a door opening. The whitewashed walls only had one set of bars, which acted as a door. It also meant that he was only able to see the visitor when she came in front of them.

Emotions of shock, disbelief, and horror flitted across his face as he stared into the storm gray eyes of the one person he thought he could rely on. There, on the other side of the bars, stood Morrigan.

Questions streamed through Jason's mind but in the end, he only asked one.

"Why?" he asked, standing up, unable to look away from her.

She returned his gaze.

"Duty called." Her voice sounded stiff.

"I thought I could trust you."

"That was a mistake."

"Everything you said last night was a lie, wasn't it?"

Morrigan looked away.

"Not everything," she whispered, her voice full of sadness.

Jason understood then. He had vaguely heard her final answer, but sleep had claimed him too soon.

Slowly, he stepped forward, reached through the bars and took her hand. She looked at him and didn't let go. The sound of footsteps on wooden stairs neared, and Morrigan pulled away. Two men came and unlocked the cell. They bound Jason's wrists and put a sack on his head. Jason was led into the unknown.

A short while later, the sack was tugged from Jason's head and he found himself in a chamber filled with people. In the center of the room was a raised dais. Standing atop it was the most beautiful woman he had ever seen. Her hair was the color of starlight, and her eyes were the purest black. The woman raised her hand and silence fell over the audience.

"Jason Lupus," she said. "Many years ago, your family cheated sacred land from us, and since that day, we have vowed to eradicate them. You are the last of your line, and, as the leader of this murder of crows, I sentence you to death!"

The crowd surged forward, people changing to huge, monstrous crows.

Jason tried to move but was held in place by Corvus and Rawkh.

Morrigan, who had been standing by the door, took a step forward, crying, "You promised him a fair trial!"

The audience cawed at her, jeering in their avian forms.

"You have become just like your mother, little half-crow," the leader spat. "There will be no trial!"

The giant crows lifted into the air, swirling into a giant black curtain that ringed the entire chamber. The leader lifted her hand and a pool of energy appeared in it.

"No!" Morrigan screamed, as the leader pulled back her arm, condensing the energy into a crackling blue bolt of lightning, and hurled it at Jason.

As the bolt of energy arced toward Jason, Morrigan leapt forward and began to change, her body shifting into that of a common raven. Morrigan shot toward Jason, racing the lightning, turning back into a human in time to shove Jason out of Corvus and Rawkh's grasp.

The bolt of lightning hit her in the chest, and she fell. As she hit the floor, all the magic that had been protecting the crows and their stronghold exploded outward in a blinding flash. All traces of the civilization were wiped out in an instant, leaving only two survivors, a boy whose life had been saved by the act of another, and a girl whose life was slipping away because of it.

Jason scrambled up and staggered to where Morrigan lay. When he saw her and saw the damage the magic had caused, he fell to his knees and gathered her up in his arms.

"Morrigan," he whispered, eyes filling with tears.

Her hand grasped his and, through the tears, he managed to see her fingers intertwined with his own.

"They were cursed," she murmured, eyes closed. "If they ever killed one of their own, the entire race would fall."

"Please don't go." Jason whispered.

"Sometimes it's good to leave something behind," she breathed. "Let me go."

Sobbing softly, Jason nodded. Morrigan breathed once, twice, and then lay still. Slowly, her body disappeared.

"Goodbye, Morrigan," Jason said.

Epilogue

Jason sat behind the check-in desk at the Wanderer's Rest. Three years earlier, shortly after leaving All Spirits Forest, he had come back to the inn and asked for a job. Kaylee, the owner and the woman who had kindly fed and housed him, agreed.

Outside, it was raining, and the inn was empty. It was about four o'clock when someone finally came in. Jason looked up to greet whoever had come in and his jaw dropped. There standing in front of him, her multicolored hair cut short, was Morrigan.

"Hello, Jason," she said.

One moment, Jason was behind the counter and the next he held Morrigan in a tight embrace.

"How are you here?" he breathed.

"Well, I had a little chat with Death and he let me come back," she answered. "Although, if you crush me to death, I doubt I'll be allowed to come back again."

Jason laughed despite being close to tears. Grabbing a key from the basket on the desk and handing it to her he said, "You better tell me everything that happened, or so help me, I just might."

Morrigan laughed as he led her into the common room and realized that she had found someone who she could tell the truth to. Her past had no control over her future.

THE FALCON'S EGG

BY ROYA TALEBREZA-MAY

Ridgeline Montessori Public Charter School

Chapter 1: Introduction

On a cool summer day, a falcon named Lilly had her first three babies. She was very excited! The third baby's first word was "adventure." Unfortunately, their tree kept having to be cut down because it was in danger of falling on a temple.

The next day when her mother went to go get food, the falcons fell into the temple because of a strong wind that capsized their branch. When their mom came back, she noticed that her little ones were not there. She looked all around the nest for them but could not find them anywhere. Little did she know her babies were inside the temple.

Unfortunately, only one baby survived the fall. Her name was Pipi the Third. Her mom was never able to find her.

Fortunately, Pipi knew of an owl named Rosemary who would definitely take her in as a family member. But when Pipi arrived, she could not find Rosemary anywhere, so she had to sleep outside, which she didn't really like.

Chapter 2: The Journey Begins

When Rosemary returned the next day, she found Pipi. She was very surprised to see Pipi, and she asked her why she was there so early in the morning. So, Pipi told Rosemary the whole story. When she finished, Rosemary welcomed her as a family member and they cooked Pipi's favorite foods almost every day.

One fine evening, the two friends thought they heard a *thud thud thud* so they decided to find the source. Little did they know it was a humongous and magical Jack Rabbit luring them in with its loud footsteps.

Since they didn't know, they set off on an adventure to find the source of the noise. They started by going to the Haunted Skull Forest, where they found lots of skeletons, but since it was haunted, they didn't stay there for very long.

The thumping got louder and led them to the HooverVille pond. It was frozen and suddenly the thumping stopped! They had a conversation and talked about where they should go. They decided on Astonish Field, but before that they had to have dinner!

They were eating beef and noodles when a Weasel named Haspairages smelled the delicious food and asked to join them. The friends decided she could, and they all made the decision that, for dessert, they would have mango-flavored snow cones! Afterward, Haspairages began tagging along, so Pipi asked her to join them on the adventure.

It was late, so they decided to sleep at a town on the way, called HooverVille. They got out their sleeping bags and tent and then they slept for fifteen hours.

When they woke up, they traveled to Astonish Field where they found five horses, but they only took three of them because that's all they needed. It felt so good to have a break from walking. But their horses were out of control, so they were forced to go wherever the horses wanted to go!

Chapter 3: The Battle

I think they ended up somewhere around Asia. They had started in the States so they somehow made it across the ocean. They also became better at steering the horses. The sights were awesome and beautiful. Once Rosemary even caught some pigs. They made bacon for breakfast. It was delicious. They also found cilantro and then, at lunch, they made cilantro soup.

But then, suddenly, a magic Jack Rabbit came and attacked them. It was coming for Pipi. but one by one, all the animals of Asia surrounded Pipi, not turning towards her but towards the rabbit. She wondered why about 9,000 animals that she barely knew were standing up for her defense. Then she realized that they were her old friends. She caught one of their eyes and winked. He winked back immediately because it was their old sign for "thank you" and "you're welcome."

By the way, if you wanted to know, Rosemary and Haspairages went to get some fish for dinner.

Chapter 4: The Celebration

When the battle ended and Rosemary and Haspairages returned, Pipi had so much to tell them that she nearly left parts out. Then, finally when Pipi finished, they had dinner. The fish were awesome but this time for dessert they only got one warhead, but it was fine because they were already pretty full from the salmon!

The next day, Pipi woke up in what looked like her tent, but it was a little different. She decided to say thank you to her new/old friends. but when she got out, she could not find Rosemary or Haspairages anywhere. She decided that they were getting stuff for breakfast, so she just went on her way.

When she arrived at their shelter, she found a wall of trees. When she tried to climb the trees they threw her off.

She decided that she could try again the next day and tried to go back to her tent, but when she got to the tent spot where it should have been, it was gone. She decided to go back to the wall to try again but when she arrived, she could not find the wall anywhere!

She decided that whoever had made the wall had taken pity and responsibility, so she just walked through the gate and guess what, in place of the door she found a banner that said, "YOU ARE THE BEST! P.S. YOU ARE KIND OF A SUCKY FIGHTER." Pipi felt annoyed, mad, and happy all at the same time!

When she got inside, she saw more signs printed in various colors such as yellow, blue, green, and orange. They all looked great, but especially the yellow and orange. They all said different things like, "Welcome back!!" or, "YOU'RE AWESOME!" or even "YOU ROCK!"

She thought it was kind of weird that her friends were throwing a party for her when they were the ones who had saved her life, but she didn't really care. She then realized that the wall was to keep her out. They were preparing, so the trees were keeping her out, because they wanted it to be a surprise. She did wonder where her real tent was, but she decided that she would figure that out later. For now, she would have some fun.

They decided the first thing they would do was take turns telling each other what they had been doing. When that conversation ended, they had tea in beanbag chairs. Finally, after that they went home.

Chapter 5: The Adventure Resumes

Pipi was already ready for another adventure, and she convinced her friends to go to a national park called Joshua Tree.

It had a lot of coyotes and mountains and canyons, and, of course, Joshua trees.

When they arrived, they decided to go to a mountain called Tree-Qwato. It was awesome, but then a roadrunner called Peppermint attacked, or at least they thought it attacked. Apparently, it was just giving a suffocating hug and now they had red marks on their necks. Despite that, they got along pretty well, and they became best friends!

Epilogue

The next day Pipi had seven babies, Peppermint had two babies and Rosemary had one baby, and they all told their children never to set up a home next to a temple! They also told their children to try to go on an adventure and defeat Troy or really just anything wild like that!

The End

To the Ends of the Earth
by Brianna R. Bird

Springfield High School

All I had was a very fluffy white cat and a scimitar. I supposed it was probably the best they could do, but when I saw the one she had, I felt very outdated.

The girl's weapon had all the bells and whistles of something of 1367—not near the beauty of mine, of course. She was wearing a very strange ensemble: a black tailcoat over a blouse tucked into brown trousers, a satchel, and her fiery hair in a braid around her head with the strangest pieces of machinery stuck into it, as well as in her buttonholes, jewelry, and belt.

I really did feel ancient in my blue and gold tunic. I hoped my back wasn't acting up again. It had been so embarrassing, getting stuck in that chimney in Mesopotamia; things weren't retractable until after that.

Anyway, she held a blunderbuss-turned-bayonet, making me look as though I had arrived at the Trojan War holding a butter knife. I flipped my hair over my other eye to get a better look at her. Her eyes were strange, it was like staring into a black pit, but her irises held flames. Of course, I surely looked strange to her.

She didn't notice me until the cat started meowing; I had poked its tail while trying to remove it from my chest. I jumped up as soon as she saw me, and carefully removed the cat. She grinned at me, and then started to walk away.

"Wait!"

I have no clue why I thought I should try to stop her, maybe because she was the only one who might be able to understand me. The other thing that surprised me was that she actually did stop.

She turned and looked at me.

"For what?"

I looked around for the first time to see we were in a rundown train station. The marble columns next to us were beautiful but looked like they had begun their completion of the dust-to-dust cycle. The eastern wall was open to the platform, where she was heading.

I blinked a couple of times, flustered.

"Where are we?"

She grinned again.

"I haven't the slightest idea."

I racked my thoughts for something more original.

"Where do I know you from?"

"I was hoping you'd be able to tell me."

"Who are you?"

"I don't think you really want to know."

She inspected my eyes in a way that was reassuring, like saying, "Don't worry, I'm the hero and I've got this," before turning again.

"But I do!"

I didn't know why I was so desperate. I tried to think. The thing was, when I searched my brain, the only thing I found was the unsettling sensation that had been descending around me for the past five minutes. I found nothing.

I realized with agonizing certainty that I knew only three things. I suspected she had landed in similar circumstances. I slung the cat over my shoulder and sprinted towards her.

"Please. I don't know what to do." I left off, not wanting to admit the bitter truth. "I don't remember anything."

She nodded enthusiastically, before giving me that look again.

"Neither do I. We might as well make introductions. I'm Achlys, and the last clear thing I remember is that I'm a daemon."

I clutched the feline against me, trying not to let Achlys see my horror. I knew I recognized her from somewhere, but I never thought it would have been the war. I inhaled deeply though my nose and tried not to focus on her hellish pupils burning into mine.

"The name's Auriel, and funnily enough, I happen to be an angel."

"So, do you know how we got here?"

I spoke timidly, the last clear thing I remembered is that everything had been greatly in turmoil in the heavens. "I think I've been sent to search for something."

Achlys was standing at the edge of the platform.

"Do you think we're searching together?" she wondered. "Or are we just racing to the trophy?"

I was put off by her light tone. My voice felt so much less confident compared to hers.

"I suppose . . . I suppose I thought that, being the only celestial beings and everything, we were simply destined to be partners."

Achlys stood watching the train tracks. They hung like Babylonian gardens over a deep chasm of mountains and valleys that I couldn't see beyond. The longer I stared, I felt a sense of unease creeping up from the depths.

"Have you figured out where we are yet?" she asked. "I think it's the answer to your question."

I look around again. There was just a platform, decaying columns, and the train tracks. Then I looked up, and I remembered where I came from.

Earth, Gaea, whatever you care to call it, was suspended perhaps ten feet from me. I could see the milky way ringed about everything like a layer of mist, circling below the mountains, with stars catching on their peaks. The sun was eclipsed by the large mass of Earth in front of us, but I could see the other planets crowning it in the background. Clouds were circling it, some of which I realized had snagged themselves on the tops of the columns, and then I remembered absolutely everything: home.

I could feel their wings brush mine. I remembered it all, our first battle, and the way they dragged my emaciated form past the gates, the way I had lain for so long in front of the garden that I thought the grass had grown over me and the moss had filled my wounds. I remembered the waterfall, and the feeling of drowning in silence, and then the relief.

I remembered it all so vividly, my books and my friends and my favorite flavors of tea that we would drink after the battles, healing ourselves with remembrance of all that is good, and the way it felt to fall asleep with my wings wrapped around my eyes and the smell of ambrosia growing beneath my branch.

I could hear Michael's voice in my ear, "I believe that they are weak when they see our love." And I could feel the wind in my hair as I sailed down through the spirals and onion domes of the most magnificent temples. I remembered it, the fellowship, the color of the dirt in my garden, the way the sun looked dark compared to our assemblies. It was home.

"This is the in-between part, isn't it?"

"Purgatory?" Achlys nodded. "I imagine what you're seeing must be better than what I'm seeing."

She was still staring down between the train tracks. I followed her gaze, but no matter how much I stared, all I saw was darkness. It hurt my eyes. She sighed.

"They wouldn't have sent us to the no man's land if they didn't want us to work together."

"What's it like down there? Why did they send us?" The questions escaped before I could stop them.

"I don't think you'd be able to understand," she said ruefully. "And us? We're the youngest. We won't hate each other as much, I suppose."

Achlys smirked at my right foot. I realized that there was a set of claws in my boot; the white cat had begun to scratch its paws against the material.

"Hey! That's sacred leather from the Holy Land!"

I hung the cat around my shoulders.

Achlys laughed as it batted at my sheath of hair.

"You've got a little parasite."

I glared at her. "How in the heavens did you get to have a bag?"

She grinned.

"Devil wears Prada and Coach. I'm surprised I don't have an Apple watch." She had a point. "No actually, I just like to keep my plans hidden. Part of the job description."

At that moment, a train car pulled into the station. Achlys alighted inside the compartment.

"Well?" Achlys asked. "Listen, angel, you've got about five seconds."

I felt anxiety crippling me. Suddenly, a very strange white form obscured my vision, and before I knew it, the cat had bounded onto the train.

"You little leviathan," I muttered, grasping for its tail.

I was too slow. I was going to fall to the ground and end

my immortal lifespan crushed beneath the wheels of a train in some devil's plot. But then there were two hands catching mine. I felt myself pulled through the door with inhuman strength as our transportation departed from the station.

Achlys released my hands, bending to stroke the cat.

"It needs a name," she remarked. "I think it looks like a Pandora."

"I was thinking something along the lines of Judah."

"Of course you were." Achlys snickered. "What about Leviathan? You did accuse it of being such."

"Pandora? Wasn't she . . ." I racked my brains for the account I'd heard from Aristotle back in the 300s. "Wasn't she the first woman?"

The flames flared in Achlys's eyes.

"She made it all go wrong. Like Eve." She thought for a moment. "I think that's why we're here. To make it go right. If we can stop Eve . . ." She trailed off. "We can stop the fall. Do you think . . ." her voice was breathless. "Do you think I can get my home back?"

I remembered what Seraph told me: "Once you're down, you're down."

But I thought it didn't work like that.

"I don't know," I said. "But what you see down there, I know that I don't want it for anyone."

The train ground to a halt. I had fallen asleep, and Leviathan had its head resting on my arm. Achlys lay on her back, and I realized I could see her dreams. Red clouds hovered over her scalp. The clouds shifted and I saw a face. Achlys, bending over a stream. Then her face vanished, and I realized I was looking through her eyes.

Two angels fought in the middle of an agora. One of them had wings that were growing holes. I watched as the

     Winners Anthology

tattered angel fell to the ground, and the other raised a sword above the first.

"Please!" Achlys shrieked. "Don't hurt her!"

I was surprised to see the angel she spoke to was Seraph.

"You're only a child," he snarled. "What would you know of these sins?"

Achlys screamed as Seraph struck the ground beside the fallen angel.

"To Hell with you, Lucifer!" he howled.

Achlys seized Lucifer's hands before she plummeted into the abyss.

"What have you done?" Achlys whispered. "I thought you said we'd be beautiful."

Seraph pulled her off of Lucifer, who fell into the dark abyss, wings tearing from her as she sank.

Seraph hissed into Achlys's ear. "Thieves. Do you know what you search for?" There was malice in his eyes. "Your greed for knowledge is the root of your evil."

Achlys was desperate. I saw her wings beginning to tear.

"Creation! That's what we were told to do!"

"You steal from your own creator, you dishonored half-breeds."

With that, Seraph shoved her. Achlys dropped through the abyss to the cold, hard nothingness. She stared as paradise closed over her.

Achlys awoke, gasping. Then a look of the deepest, darkest shame that I have only ever seen in the eyes of one other person came into her eyes. It was the same look the man wore when he wrapped his fist around a bag of silver pieces.

The train door rolled open. We stood on a wasteland between two rivers, the trunks of dead trees and abandoned fountains surrounded us.

"What did you mean?" I hesitated, not wanting to offend her. "You said that if we succeed, you might get your home back?"

"Do you know why we are here?"

"We're here to stop the end of the world, aren't we?"

"We can delay it. We have to go back to Eden."

I stared at her.

"You mean, you can't possibly mean that you want to . . . You want to stop Lucifer?"

She nodded. I stared at her in awe.

"You can't do this. I have to be the one." Achlys spoke quickly, as if the words would escape her if she didn't voice them. "Your side gave mine a choice, and I need to stop them." Her eyes flicker. "We weren't given free will to sabotage ourselves. It's time I redeemed myself."

With that, she did the thing I least expected. She took my hand.

"You saw my dreams. I just wanted to create, away from people like Seraph. He just controlled. We wanted freedom. But Lucifer was different. She destroyed." She took a slow breath again. "I never wanted to hurt anyone. This is my battle to fight."

With that, Achlys seized both my hands and I felt as though I were falling down, down, down. I could see layers of time peeling off the landscape. We fell through thousands of years.

And then, we were there. And there was a dragon standing before us, its wings beating the branches of a tree bearing golden apples.

I could see, across the plains of bushes and trees, two brilliantly beautiful people walking across the lawns. They were holding each other's hands and laughing, their hair blowing around each other like clouds around mountains.

"I'm going after her."

The pupils in Achlys's irises were glowing, and sparks were raining down her cheeks. Was she . . . crying?

"I don't know what's going to happen to me, but I want it to be worth something."

Then she was running away from me, her hair falling loose from its braid and spilling around her shoulders. I tried to follow her on foot, but I was too slow. She was running through a stream leading to a waterfall, and at the top of the waterfall stood the gilded apple tree.

Achlys wouldn't get up the cliffs in time without help. I relaxed all my muscles, closed my eyes, and pictured sunlight and birds and the feeling of wind whooshing through ruffled feathers. And then there they were: a pair of wings resting on my shoulder blades.

I soared across the lawn, and quickly caught up to her. I grasped her under the arms and hoisted her up the waterfall, dropped her on the bank, and then flew towards the people making their way across the grass.

I landed in front of them, my wings still outstretched. They stared at me in shock, and for a moment I was at a loss for words. What was the thing Michael always said?

"Don't be afraid!" I stammered. "Everything's all right."

They still looked afraid. Michael hadn't gone over what to do when that happened.

"Well, mostly, that is!" I started again, taking a deep breath. "Listen; I can't change fate. But I can give you a warning. In a matter of moments, you are going to be given a choice that will alter all of human nature and their future for the rest of history."

They still looked scared.

"I cannot stop you. But I can give you advice. Remember all that you have been given, remember who you are. Remember your love for one another."

A scream pierced the air. I whipped around to see Achlys being lifted into the air, and I began to rise from the ground. I looked back at the couple one more time.

"Be strong. Be wise. We're all counting on you."

I soared towards the tree, where Achlys was now astride the dragon's back. She had her gun pointed towards its heart, and her other hand was pressed against her side. I flew forward. An enormous claw batted at me, but I dove down toward Achlys. She gasped as I placed my scimitar in her hand, and I took the blunderbuss and began to riddle the hide of the serpent with bullet holes.

A tremendous roar nearly flayed our flesh as the dragon's claw fell from its body; Achlys had cut herself free. And with another sweep of the scimitar, the dragon was crashing towards the ground. Achlys was nowhere to be seen, and I realized in horror that she was buried beneath the monstrous corpse.

I flew forwards, screaming her name. She couldn't be gone, she had lived through too much. The monster had caused an enormous crater, and I realized that it was all sinking into the ground.

I hurtled towards the ground, thinking that I would surely collide with the earth, until I realized that the monster had plummeted underground. And then it struck me—I was plummeting straight into Hell.

Despair filled me. I had to turn back. But there she was; I caught sight of Achlys's form falling deep into the black cavern below. I couldn't leave her like this. I beat my wings together and accelerated faster than I thought possible. And then, suddenly, I caught her arm in mine, and was dragging her back into the light.

Achlys was so limp in my arms, at first I thought her dead, but I felt a faint flutter of her heart against my neck. Where was I taking her? Would they let her back? I could confront Seraph, plead her case before the Divine, but suddenly I felt her tugged away from me.

I shrieked as I felt her sliding down out of the sky. She was two feet below me, now three feet—

And then Achlys was beside me again in the clouds, and she was glowing. The sun was glinting off her mane of fiery curls, and her irises were golden. But most beautiful of all, a pair of golden wings beat the air behind her. She was rising with me into the heavens.

"How—" I started.

She cut me off. "We did it!"

"No, you did it." I grabbed her hands. "Come on! I want to take you home!"

And then we were flying hand in hand through the vast expanse of blue, with two shining gates unfolding above us.

Sweet Dreams Are Made of This

Gold Dust Books

by L. Stepp

Creswell High School

This wasn't how it was supposed to be. This wasn't how life was supposed to go. I wasn't supposed to spend my life sitting in the office of a job I didn't even want. I was meant to be doing something better. Something that had meaning and made me feel like I led a fulfilling and rewarding life.

My mother had raised me on fairy tales and stories. Stories that had been told to her when she was young. Stories that she could create on the spot, that were filled with adventure. We were kissing frogs, dancing until midnight, fighting evil witches, and becoming apprentices to eccentric wizards. We were making friends with knights and ninjas, fighting to save whoever needed saving.

I grew to believe that anything could happen. We could be the ones to tame dragons. We could be the ones to save a kingdom. We could be the ones to do anything. Someday, something would happen that would change our lives for the better, we just had to wait a little longer. As the years passed, nothing as amazing as what happened in the stories occurred.

I was getting older, growing up faster and faster. My mother and I were still reading the same stories that we had when I was little. They still held the same amount of magic and adventure as ever.

My mother was getting older, too, and I started reading on my own. I read and dreamed up my own adventures. I climbed up castle walls, I got into brawls in taverns, and was thrown through windows. I met forest spirits and wonderful creatures that couldn't be found outside of the pages of books. I fell in love time and time again and my heart was broken just as many times.

Those that I had grown to care for died in front of me over and over. I lost count of the ones I had lost. But I always remembered them. I knew their names, their thoughts, and their opinions. I knew them, and I cried for them.

I cried for them in the darkness of the night as the memories of all they had been through and accomplished throughout their book swirled through my mind.

But I still hoped; hoped that something would change and I would find myself flying through the night sky on the back of a dragon beside those I had lost.

I spent the following years alone for the most part. I decided to quit my job and go back to school. I looked for a part-time job close to campus. It was while I was looking that I discovered a small bookshop.

The shop was a hidden gem in the bustling downtown of my city. Most people didn't realize that it was even there. The brickwork of the building stood out from the pristine glass walls of its neighbors, and yet, most who wandered by didn't care to find out what was inside. One would think that the building would be easily noticed due to how different it was from the rest of the street.

That's what I thought anyway, as that was what had drawn my attention in the first place.

The large blue "Closing Sale!" sign in the window stood out starkly against the warm browns of the aged brick.

"I'm getting old, dear. I can't take care of this place like I used to," the old woman who owned the shop sighed. "This place used to be bursting with people. Quiet Sunday teas and extravagant late afternoon parties."

Her eyes were distant, watching the memories replay in her mind, and I was watching with her.

The tall walls filled from top to bottom with books. The winding staircase in the back corner led to two balconies of different heights that circled the room above my head. There was light streaming in through the windows near the ceiling, natural spotlights shining on the floor where the golden ghosts swayed to softly playing music.

Plush couches framed the room and well-dressed men and women were lounging as the Grand Opening Party of The Book Nook continued to progress.

The room felt almost like a forest: potted plants with long winding vines that reached towards the floor and lower balcony were scattered along the windowsills; wood furniture and bookcases with accents of different shades of green surrounded the room, while the smell of pine drifted by on the breeze of a dancing couple.

The woman turned back to me with a soft smile and a sad look in her eyes.

"If only you could have been there. Felt what it was like," she sighed.

Around me, the dancing couples and lounging ladies faded out. Nothing but the faint smell of pine was left as the woman's memory faded.

I stood there for a few minutes, soaking in the fading sights. I returned every day after that and spent a few hours looking through the amazing collection of books the room held.

Over time I started helping the old woman. I dusted the shelves, swept the floors, watered the plants, and every single moment I was happy. I felt at peace for the first time in a long time.

I started reading the stories that my mother had told me again. I could feel these stories come to life within the walls of the shop. There seemed to be a shift in the atmosphere, the building felt more free, more alive.

I stayed longer every time I visited.

The blue "Closing Sale'" sign stayed in the window, slowly fading in color and collecting dust. But the shop had never once been closed when I passed by, and I would often find myself sitting in one of the many armchairs with a book in my hand.

I wasn't always reading. Sometimes I would sit and listen to the memories that filled the place. The golden shadows of men and women in beautiful coats and dresses with the characteristics of the Belle Époque were laughing across the room, gossiping about the latest party they had attended. There was always something happening in this place. So many memories.

Memories from the Grand Opening Party of The Book Nook. Memories from when the old woman's husband bought the shop from an even older widow. Memories from before, when The Book Nook had been Rose Family Books. Memories that only a few could see and hear in the golden light cast through the windows high above.

There was peace here. Calm. I felt like I could spend the rest of my life in this place.

It was two years before I found that I could spend the rest of my life here if I wished. The old woman passed and gifted me the shop as well as a small fortune to keep the doors open for those who stumbled by. I spent my life running the shop without ever having to worry about closing down or needing to find other work. I surrounded myself with the wonders and faded memories that filled the building.

I invited my mother to come live with me in the small apartment behind the shop. We lived there for a few more years before my mother followed the old woman and passed as well.

Though in that time we had together, we created more memories to add to the gold shadows. A grand re-opening party was thrown in celebration of a new name and new management. Sunday teas were set and book clubs met. Birthdays and game nights were had. I met my first love and suffered many break-ups. My wedding was celebrated within the walls of the newly named Gold Dust Books.

They weren't just our memories. Our family grew. Regulars in the shop became friends and family over the years. People we shared our stories and ideas with. Customers who found themselves unexpectedly walking through the doors on a rainy day looking for something magical.

It took time but eventually, golden shadows came out of hiding, mesmerizing those able to see them. Children and adults alike watched history unfold from within the brickwork of the building. Imprints from those who had walked before us and with us.

My time would come in the end, as it has now. I find you wandering through the door with a faded blue "Closing Sale" sign in its window. You tell me about the stories your mother told you when you were younger. How you wanted to be a superhero or a pirate who sailed the seas looking for gold.

I whisper, "You have."

You turn your head as a sparkle of gold catches your attention from the corner of your eye, and you watch as the memories unfold in front of you, waiting for you to make your own.

SECRET RECIPE
BY JOCELYNE STEVENSON

Pleasant Hill Elementary School

"Anne, come help me cook!" hollered Mom from the kitchen.

"On my way," Anne yelled back.

It was November twenty second and Thanksgiving was around the corner. That also meant all of her family members were too.

Anne had so much family, it was troublesome to count! She had Aunt Tracey, Aunt Stacey, Aunt Macey, Uncle Jerry, Uncle Trey, Uncle Larry, Uncle Steve, Grandpa Victor, Grandpa Matt, Grandma Jane, Grandma Belle, and all of her older and younger cousins. They were cooking food for the traditional Thanksgiving family dinner that happened every single year.

Anne thought the only good part of Thanksgiving was the pumpkin pie. Anne loved the creamy, velvety texture of the delicacy. Every year, her mom baked the scrumptious treat with her dad, Grandma Jane, and Aunt Tracey. Her mom said she'd show the recipe to her when she turned twenty. Mom's secret recipe always awed her. Every Thanksgiving she begged her mother for it, but she always said no. This Thanksgiving it would change.

She finished brushing her teeth and slid on her pajamas. It was Thanksgiving eve and she had a plan. When the clock struck midnight, she'd find that pesky piece of paper. She tiredly reached for her alarm clock and set it for 11:55 pm before shutting her eyes and burying herself in her comforter.

Ring, ring, ring! Her alarm buzzed and vibrated. She reached up and turned it off as quickly as possible, in order not to wake up her little brother Joseph, whom she unfortunately shared a room with.

It was 11:56 pm and she needed to be in the kitchen by twelve o'clock. Silently, she tiptoed to the door and carefully turned the knob. She crept through the hallway like a ninja. When she finally got past the upstairs bathroom, she attempted the creaky, squeaky, wooden stairs. On one step, she nearly fell and twisted.

"Yikes," she thought to herself.

This would be a lot harder than it seemed.

Step by step, cautious not to make any sound, Anne descended each stair. When she reached downstairs, she had to have to face the hardest task of them all. Anne had to cross by her parents' bedroom door. It was going to be extremely difficult as her dad was easily awoken, and her mom frequently got up for water and midnight snacks.

Anne took a deep breath in and changed her mind set to a burglar sneaking through her very own house. She decided it was best to army crawl along the flat wooden floor because it would make no sound. After several seconds of careful crawling, she made it into the kitchen. She had an idea of where the recipe might be hidden, but it was a risky attempt because she would need to climb an unstable stool.

She checked the pantry and found nothing. She checked all the cabinets for it but found nothing. She checked everywhere, even the oven and fridge, but still found nothing. Not even a trace of where it could be.

She was about to give up when she stepped on the mat in front of the kitchen sink and heard a crackling sound. She checked to see what it was and, to her surprise, it was the homemade pumpkin pie recipe!

She never thought an old worn-out piece of yellow paper would make her this happy, but it did. She cheered silently so she wouldn't wake her dad up. She padded to the dining room as silent as a mouse. Not even her pet cat, Simba, could hear her.

In the darkness, she continued, optimistically hoping she was going the right way, as it had gotten darker as the little light that shone on the stovetop had gotten dimmer the farther she walked from it. She was nearly there when she stepped on Simba. He violently hissed and growled so loudly Anne worried her parents would hear him.

And, like a fortune teller, Anne's dad stormed from his bedroom to the living room, too tired to be furious at her. He snatched the recipe out of his daughter's hand and sent Anne to her bedroom. Wiping a tear from her eye, Anne changed her alarm to 8:00 am, closed her eyes, and fell asleep with anger and exasperation.

Anne woke up the next morning before her alarm. She took a shower, made her bed, brushed her teeth, and got dressed. Then she woke up Joseph for Thanksgiving. Anne wasn't in the mood to fight about him getting up so she simply took his pillow and blanket and put them somewhere he couldn't reach. Then, she cleaned her room and wrote an apology note for her parents. She scurried downstairs to find her mom looking disappointed in her. Her father was still sleeping, so he wasn't in on the conversation.

"You know you're not supposed to take stuff from me without my permission. And you also know that you're never allowed to leave your room after you're sent to bed, only to get water, use the restroom, or inform me about an emergency. I accept your apology, but your pumpkin pie privileges have been taken away from you this Thanksgiving," Anne's mom explained.

"But Mom!" she protested.

Anne ran back up to her room, lividly slamming the door. She could tell this Thanksgiving was going to be bad.

Finally, all her aunts, uncles, grandpas, grandmas, and cousins came to the celebration.

Aunt Macey brought her signature mashed potatoes, Grandpa Matt brought his famous turkey, and her mom brought her delectable pumpkin pie. Everyone sat down at the extra-large Thanksgiving table and chowed down.

Since Anne was banned from her favorite dessert, she tried Grandma Belle's asparagus and found it OK. Then she tried her cousin's fall-themed cookies and thought they were tasty. She even tried Grandpa Matt's turkey. Everything changed.

Anne realized she liked this more than the homemade pumpkin pie. She surprisingly ate the most out of everyone at the table. She enjoyed this Thanksgiving more than the rest.

When everyone left and it was time for bed, Anne brushed her teeth, dressed in her pajamas, set her alarm for 7:30 am, snuggled into her blankets, and closed her eyes in satisfaction.

THE STRENGTH OF THE WEAK

BY SIDNEY JOHNSON

Pleasant Hill Elementary School

**Chapter 1: The Hunt, or How to Suddenly
Lose Everything**

"Come on, you can't just laze off. The chickens have eggs, and the cows are giving me a look."

Kiya groaned and opened his eyes. Mia stared right back at him. Kiya smiled and sat up.

"If you could talk, you would be pretty awesome," he informed his dog as he stretched and stood up.

"Kiya, get down here!" his mom hollered.

"Oops. I'm running late," he said as Mia panted and snuggled onto his bed.

Kiya lived in the Era of Emperor Kee. Kee was a terrible emperor who treated his people like trash and was in constant debt to shifty governors. Everyone starved while he ate roasted pheasants and pomegranates.

The citizens hated him, but any who spoke ill of the emperor disappeared and were never heard from again. Most went to Kuscu, the emperor's dirty island prison, and stayed there until they died or were driven mad.

Now it was the Day of the Tested, to see who was who.

Each sixteen-year-old was sorted into the Strong or the Weak. The Strong became successful men in the military.

They became farmers, school teachers, or even guards for the emperor if they were lucky. As for the Weak, they became slaves who did the dirty work like trash collectors, sewer cleaners, maids, and cooks.

Sadly, Kiya was destined to be a Weak as he had no athletic qualities whatsoever. The testing was never based on intelligence as the intelligent might become weary of the emperor and question his ideas.

When Kiya told his mother that he was a Weak, she paled and put her hands to her mouth.

"No, it—it can't be! Oh, dear. Get your father."

Kiya ran to collect his father worriedly.

Kiya's father came in and gently held his wife while she told him the news. He gripped her tight as the news set in. Their eyes connected and held love and worry.

"But—"

"Shh. You know what."

"Danger . . ."

"I am prepared to do it."

"The stakes. . ."

"Are worth it," his mother finished.

Kiya's father nodded and turned around.

"Son."

Kiya looked up.

"Tomorrow evening you'll go into the woods with enough food and water for many days. We'll hide Mia at Cavern's Pass, but you should climb the Hillside Cliff tree. Answer to no one. Not even me or your mother. Do not move if you hear shouting or threats. Do. Not. Answer. Come down after three days and head toward your aunt's house in Swampy Hovels. And above all, stay safe. Understood?" his father asked.

Kiya nodded.

"But—but what about you and Mom? What if something happens to you?"

"We will be fine."

Kiya knew better. He saw real fear in his father's eyes. The collectors were a vicious pack of men with pistols and a hunger for despair.

* * *

THE NEXT EVENING THERE WAS A LOUD BANGING ON the door.

"It's the collectors! Run! Out the back door!" Kiya's mother shoved him a heavy sack.

"Mia's already in the caves. Go!"

Kiya paused at the backdoor.

"I—I love you," Kiya blurted out.

"I love you, too," his mother said.

"I love you three. Now go!" his father said as the banging returned more aggressively.

Kiya ran out the back as his father opened the front door. Kiya took a step toward the forest, then thought better of it and crept around the house to peek in a window. Five men in black trench coats and muddy army boots stood inside the house interrogating Kiya's parents. They were quiet until they found out Kiya was gone.

"Gone?" sneered one of the men.

"Left early in the morning. Took the dog and everything," answered his father.

"That's likely," the leader said. Then he said something to his parents and Kiya's mother paled considerably. Kiya's father took a step forward.

The leader quickly snatched Kiya's mother.

"Oh, she's pretty," he said as he put his greasy fingers on her.

Kiya's dad began to walk forward when *BANG!* He collapsed at the feet of the leader. Kiya's mother began to cry while Kiya shook. That man had just killed his father. Kiya's mother finally noticed him and mouthed one word.

"Run."

He ran.

Chapter 2: The Tree of True Seeing, or Allies Are Nice

Kiya ran through the forest, branches ripping against his arms and legs, tears blurring his vision. *How could this have happened?* He ran until he could not, until he collapsed at a tree. He looked up at the tree as a pink petal brushed his face. The Tree of True Seeing! The legend said that only the true at heart could find it at their most desperate moment. That gave him an idea. If he could climb it, he would never be found. He scrambled up its bark until he hid in the fullest leafed area. He almost relaxed until . . .

"Kiya?"

Kiya froze.

"Keeya? Kooya? This is so confusing." It was a young collector, but one he had not seen at the house.

"What a pretty tree. Nice and solid. I wish I was a tree. No screaming father. No crazy expectations," the kid sighed. "I know I'm lucky and everything, but I—I really hate it."

He sounded so heartbroken that Kiya sighed.

"Wha— Who's there? I'm armed!" The boy pulled out a dagger. Kiya barely breathed as the boy walked around the tree, looking into the forest.

"Who am I kidding, I can't even fight with one of these things." He dropped the dagger.

"I'm an utter failure. A disgrace to the Kee family."

Kiya froze. This was Emperor Kee's son!

"I don't want to be a killer!" The prince plopped down on a nearby stump.

"Maybe I could run away! But all the other lands are hostile."

And then Kiya did something so dangerous that, when he would look back on that day, he would shake his head. He spoke.

"I could help," he said.

The prince was on his feet in an instant, and then he slapped his head and sat back down.

"Hallucinations, Kyle? Get it together," he mumbled.

"No, I'm really here. I have a question for you," said hidden Kiya.

"Wait . . . The tree is talking! What is it, O magical tree?" The prince gazed in awe at the tree. Kiya stifled a snicker.

"Would you cut me down if your father wanted it? If he wanted me dead?" Kiya asked, intrigued.

"N—no. Not really. I'd find a way to fake it," Kyle answered.

"Oh, well, fine." And slowly Kiya descended until he was sitting on the bottom branch. The prince stared in awe at Kiya.

"You—you're a—a wood nymph!" he blurted out.

Kiya laughed and waved away the suggestion.

"No, Kyle. I am not a nymph. I believe you were searching for me?"

Kyle's eyes widened.

"You're my destiny?!" he gasped.

"No dude, I'm Kiya." Kiya rolled his eyes.

"Kiya? Kiya . . . wait, what!? You're Kiya? I could turn you in!" he said as his eyes lit up.

"And forever be unhappy with your life?" Kiya retorted.

"How much did you hear?" Kyle asked suspiciously.

"Enough. It seems like you have two choices. You can run

away with me to rescue my mother, or turn me in to be killed and continue your unhappy life."

Kyle struggled with the decision for just a moment.

"What the heck, I haven't got much to lose. I went from a raging father back home to a raging sergeant here in the collectors . . . so yes. Please take me." Kyle stood up as Kiya slid down the tree and smiled.

"Let's go."

Chapter 3: The Mowthrout, or Why You Should Sometimes Let Dogs Eat Random Plants

"Aroof!" Mia woofed as Kyle patted her head. Kiya chuckled as she pranced around after a butterfly.

"You know, Kyle, you really have a way with animals," Kiya said as Mia jumped into a flower bush in hot pursuit of the butterfly.

Kiya paused to look at Kyle. He was a strong kid with a stocky shape and big muscles. His black hair was in an army cut and he had a charming smile that was slightly mischievous. Kyle seemed like a softy at heart as he ran after Mia, and the two of them slipped into a mud pile.

"Need a hand?" Kiya said as he pulled Kyle up. Mia panted and flopped back into the mud.

Kyle brushed the dirt and grass off his clothes. They had been traveling for days toward the shores of the Black Sea. There they would find a boat to travel across the sea, save Kiya's mom, and then . . . who knew? They were mainly focusing on the rescue.

It was slow going. Branches cut and bruised them, thorn bushes forced them back, and ravines dotted the landscape. Finally, as they made camp during the evening, they heard a noise.

"Shh. I'll put out the fire while you get our stuff," whispered Kiya.

They grabbed Mia and hid under a rotted-out tree root. They all barely fit as they squeezed in.

"Come out, boys, there's no use hiding, I only want a kiss." A slippery voice drifted into their ears. Kiya widened his eyes and mouthed the word "Mowthrout."

In the legend, Mowthrout's were terrible demons that stalked travelers through the forest and mesmerized their prey. They would eat anyone and were vicious and disgusting. Kiya quickly covered his ears. Kyle almost put his hands up to block the sound, and then his eyes lifted as if in a dreamy haze.

"Please come out, you wouldn't want to hurt my . . . feelings." The monster's greasy voice felt like a slimy eel. Kyle slowly rose from their hiding spot.

"No, I wouldn't want that," Kyle said as he stared into the Mowthrout's gaze.

"Boy," she said in her cracked falsetto. "Come to me, my darling." She smiled. She was a vulture with gray cracked skin stretched tight with two leathery wings and one arm that had two sharp claws. Her mouth was stained red.

"Come to mama."

Kiya burst from his hiding place.

"Kyle, no!"

The vulture smiled.

"You've just assured your death, too!" She spread her massive wings and roared, "Darlings, come!"

Thousands of bats flocked down and hit Kiya with their claws, dropping dead insects and gooey stuff. From the corner of his eye, Kiya saw Mia chomping on something.

"I wish she could tell me what she's doing," he thought.

What he didn't see was a shooting star right above his head at the exact time he wished. Then Mia barked, except it came out more like "Bar—kk—away from my friends!"

Kiya fell over in shock. The Mowthrout was so surprised that she wavered and her spell broke, something that had not happened since she was a little Mowthroutling. Kyle froze and started shuddering, a common effect of surviving the spell.

"That's right! Go!"

Even Mia was surprised by her words, as usually they had little effect. But right then, they had a big effect!

The Mowthrout shrieked and flew off to find other food that didn't include talking animals. Kiya started laughing hysterically, and Kyle regained control of his body and stood up weakly.

"What the . . . WOOF . . . is happening?" Kiya cracked up.

Kyle walked over and said, "Kiya? Are you OK? And . . . Mia?"

"So they're true! Wishing plants are true!" Kiya said as he sniffed.

"Wishing plants?" Kyle asked, confused.

"It's said that anyone who eats a Wishing plant gets one wish. They are almost extinct, since traders pick them to sell. This plant is probably the only one left in the whole forest. And Mia ate it." Kiya shook his head and stood up, right as Mia burped a large purple bubble.

"Side effect," Kiya whispered.

"Uh, Kiya? I don't think I can walk much further after . . . that," Kyle said weakly.

"That's OK. We're here!" Kiya pulled back a vine to reveal a pitch-black circle of water with a tiny island on the horizon. Anchored by the shore was a boat!

Chapter 4: The Rescue, or How to Save Your Mother in THE Most Unexpected Way Possible

The sail out to Kuscu prison had been largely uneventful.

"Weird. There's no fence or anything," Kiya muttered.

"It's because they have nothing to fear," Kyle answered. "No one in their right mind would come out here."

"That makes sense. We're here because I always use my left mind instead," Kiya replied. Kyle snickered.

"Guys, someone is coming! Hide!" Mia whispered too late.

"Stop! Intruders. Wait . . . Prince Kyle? What are you doing here?" A bright flashlight beam went straight in their eyes. Suddenly Kyle straightened and spoke.

"What do you think? I'm escorting a prisoner with my guard dog," he said as he clamped a hand on Kiya's neck.

"But—but you've been missing! This is wonderful news! I must tell your fath—"

"Don't you think he knows I'm here? Let me into the prison. I shall have this child and his mother presented to my father to be hanged."

Kiya shivered at the word.

"But you'll need a guard. I can offer you my best!" The guard nodded vigorously.

"Thank you, but no. This prison is so well guarded I don't need protection. Or is it not as spectacular as I've been led to believe?"

The guard faltered for a moment.

"As you wish, my prince." He stepped away.

The boys entered through several large iron doors. A wooden sign above read "Kuscu, Prison of Despair. Welcome!"

They heard moans and cries coming from the cells as they walked deeper into the prison.

"I know where I'm going. I had a royal tour last fall," Kyle said as he turned left, then right, up a tight spiral staircase and then down a narrow corridor.

"Hey, guys?" Mia wagged her tail. "I'm getting a bad vibe down this hallway."

They could hear heavy breathing and nails scratching as something big moved toward them.

"Other way, other way!" Kyle pushed Kiya down another hall and Mia ran ahead as they heard a howl. "A Sucker. They feed on despair and sadness. No one quite knows when they came, but they just appeared in the prison and started working here."

Kyle ran down more twists and turns until he stopped.

"Prisoner 1367. Your mother."

Kiya peered in and stopped. Her beautiful long shimmery black hair was ragged and cut short.

When she saw them, she rasped, "Kiya! Oh, my dear. Why are you here? You were safe! Safe from the demons."

She started shivering uncontrollably.

"But I see you now. The angels, they're here to save me! Where's your father? Go find him, you silly boy!"

She had reached madness. "I know Papa won't like our arrangements, but he can't stop me! Don't you agree Mary? Mary!?"

Kiya stepped back.

"I'm Kiya. Not Mary," he said.

"Who's Kiya?" she said, cocking her head.

Kiya turned to Kyle.

"She—she doesn't recognize me. Mary is her sister." Kiya said, shivering.

"We have to get her out of here! I'll call for a guard to haul her and you—"

Kiya was overcome with despair and ran down the hall.

"I've lost Papa, and now I've lost Mama," he thought as he ran past the cells. Except slowly there weren't any cells, and he ran into something hard.

He looked up, expecting to find a guard or a Sucker, but it was a shrine. The shrine held two golden dragons with emerald eyes, except both were slightly askew. The words on the shrine said, "They who solve the riddle get one wish."

Kiya slowly pushed the dragons into alignment. Suddenly water erupted from the dragons' mouths and into a fountain.

"I am Eriya, Goddess of the Water. What brings you to my shrine?" A voice majestically floated from the fountain.

"Um, well, I—" Kiya began as a spirit phased out of the fountain and sat on top.

"Ah, it is you, little hero. Do you want money? All humans want money." The spirit rubbed her hands together.

"Not really, because well, my mother is mad and I don't know how we're going to survive—"

"I know! A wish and a present because I like your cause."

She snapped her fingers and *poofed* out of existence. Kiya bowed and ran back through the maze to Kyle.

"Kiya? Where are we?" Kiya's mother rubbed her head.

"Everything's all right, Mom. Just breathe."

* * *

One year later.

"Kiya come on! You have a meeting with the Emperor!" Mia yelled.

Kiya groaned and sat up.

"Well, hello to you too, Mia."

She grinned and wagged her tail. Kia threw on some clothes and ran out of his room.

"Morning, Mom!" he said as he grabbed a piece of bread and walked to the castle. After they had gotten back from the island, they had learned that Emperor Kee had died of a snake bite and Kyle was now the Emperor. Kyle had declared Kiya and his mother innocent and built them a new house next to the palace.

"How things change!" he thought as he walked. "One day I'm running from the emperor, and now I'm his bestie!" He sat down in a chair as Emperor Kyle walked in.

"Good morning, Kiya! And you too, Mia."

"Hi, Emperor Kyle!" Kiya said jokingly.

"We've talked about this, just call me Kyle."

"Righto mundo, Sir Highly Esteemed Kyle of the Land," he teased.

"Come, Kiya. Look at our beautiful city!" Kyle said.

After Kyle was appointed emperor, he dropped the sorting system and arrested many of the collectors for their crimes. People were now free to choose their own path in life.

"You know, Kiya, we may face danger and suffering. But I'll do my best to stop it." Kiya smiled and held his hand.

"You mean, we'll do it together."

And the two boys looked out over their land, a royal and an outcast, united.

Let Go

by Nina Kuhl

Roosevelt Middle School

How can this be the new reality?

Marilyn sat hunched in the back seat of her mom's silver SUV, gazing blankly out the window. Her heart began to palpitate, causing her chest to cramp, while hot sweat dripped from her palms.

"Are you OK, sweetheart?" her mother asked gently, noticing her daughter's pale, panicked face through the rearview mirror.

"I'm . . . fine," Marilyn whispered, her silvery voice sinking into the silence, barely even there.

Powerful, overwhelming emotions flooded into her brain, faster than a rapid river, drowning all thoughts of happiness and pleasant things. It was grief and fierce worry, mixed with great annoyance that she had to spend her Saturday at a therapist's office.

"I know this isn't your ideal weekend activity," Marilyn's mom admitted empathetically, sensing Marilyn's thoughts. "I understand how you feel, but, trust me, this will be good for you."

"This will be good for you." Those words weren't new to Marilyn's ears. In fact, that sentence was pretty much all her mother had said to her in the last month.

The almost-teenager didn't feel the need to respond as they pulled into a mostly empty parking lot. Every word that escaped her mouth was another useless attempt at knocking some sense into her mom.

Her body shaking involuntarily, Marilyn hesitated before exiting the car. Her insides squirmed and twisted, refusing to sit still while her head pounded with anxiety. Reluctantly, she directed herself towards a tall windowless building that eerily resembled a prison.

The mother and girl, both anxious for their own reasons, entered the gloomy building and walked into a small, colorful room with a wooden desk and a few bright cushioned chairs, the smell of jasmine immediately striking Marilyn's nostrils.

Marilyn's mom stepped up to the desk and began to speak politely to the young lady sitting there, who appeared about as bored as the kids in Marilyn's social studies class. Refusing to look her mom in the eye, Marilyn focused her gaze on her beaten-up Converse, which rested on the dusty wood floor.

After a long minute, Marilyn's mom ushered her to sit on one of the comfy chairs. Marilyn collapsed onto a pillow, settling into the peace of the room, which in no way matched the outside of the building.

Her eyes fluttered shut and her breath slowed slightly. Through all the panicked thoughts swirling around her brain, one question poked its way to the top: *Why?* Why did her mom think sending her to some rando she'd never met would cure her grief? Why did her mom think she'd benefit from confirming the fact that she had a "disorder?" Why did her mom think that this was the only solution?

Sure, Marilyn had struggled with depression ever since her father passed away a few months ago. But throwing her into a neon chair and telling her to express how she felt to an unfamiliar woman was not how to solve that problem.

The low, gravelly voice of a middle-aged man jerked Marilyn back to sad reality.

"Marilyn Clements?"

"All right, honey, that's you!" Marilyn's mom whispered, giving her daughter a light push.

"I know my name," Marilyn hissed back, swallowing her nerves and gingerly following the man as he led her down a dark hallway.

His cold, stern face certainly did not make Marilyn feel more at ease as he gestured toward the end of the hall where a cozy little office lay ahead of them.

"Dr. Katz will be there in a minute," the guy told Marilyn in his gruff voice. "You can go inside and wait till she comes."

"OK," Marilyn stuttered inaudibly as the man marched off, leaving her alone, like she had been for the past two-and-a-half months.

It was awkward standing in the hallway by herself, so Marilyn followed instructions and walked into the little pink office. It looked like it had been decorated by a cat lady who was obsessed with the color pink. Everything was either furry, fuzzy, or fluffy. Pink paintings of flowers and kittens lined the walls, fairy lights and artificial pink ivy dangled from the ceiling, a soft pink rug spread across the floor, and the cushioned chairs and couch were covered in heart-shaped pillows and the kind of squishy stuffed animals that little kids squeeze when they're upset. Marilyn took a seat on the big fluffy couch and let her thoughts fill the silence.

She couldn't do this. No matter how much her mom wanted it. It wasn't fair and it didn't feel right. This wouldn't help—it would make everything worse.

"Sorry, Mom," Marilyn mumbled as she rose to her feet and made a beeline for the door.

It seemed that it was clearly not Marilyn's lucky day. Just as her hand gripped the door handle, a blonde lady briskly walked up to the door as well, causing Marilyn's cheeks to turn pink and rush back to the cushy couch, just as the lady pushed open the door.

The woman entered the office and strolled over to the heavily decorated desk in the corner. She took a seat in the rolling chair and grinned as she said jokingly, "I hope you weren't trying to run away. Don't worry. I don't bite."

Marilyn just stared at her, not daring to answer. The lady looked like she was in her thirties (as predicted), her shoulder-length hair falling around her dimpled cheeks and her warm turquoise eyes sparkling at Marilyn.

"Hi there, it's very nice to meet you," the woman said as she settled into her chair and opened her desktop computer. "I'm Dr. Katz, and it seems like I'll be working with you for a little bit. I assume you're Marilyn?"

Ignoring all desperate wishes to leave, Marilyn forced her head to nod.

Dr. Katz beamed another pearly white smile.

"Great! So, Marilyn, I just want to let you know before we begin that this is a very safe place. Whatever you choose to say will stay between you and me—I won't tell anyone else anything, not even your parents or family. The only exception is if you say something that suggests potential danger for yourself or others—for example, if you were to talk about a plan to injure yourself, or someone else. Understood?"

Another reluctant nod from Marilyn.

"Awesome! Also remember that you can share anything you like, and I promise not to respond negatively. I won't make fun of you or say anything judgmental. I'm only here to help you."

Marilyn didn't respond, so Dr. Katz continued.

"On that note, let's get started! So, Marilyn, how old are you?"

"Twelve."

"Such a great age. And are you in sixth or seventh grade?"

"Seventh."

There wasn't anything Marilyn hated more than peppy adults who try to coat everything they say with an extra layer of sugar. It was so obviously fake and annoying—couldn't Dr. Katz just say the facts: "There's something wrong with your brain. I'm here to make you normal like everyone else."

"How's that going for you so far? Do you have friends at school?'

What kind of question was that? Did she have friends? Of course she had friends. Did she really seem that pathetic?

"Yes," Marilyn grunted.

"OK, just checking in! Do you have a good friend group? Or just a couple close friends?"

"I have a group."

"Wonderful! Do you get along with your family? What is it like at home?"

"My dad just died." Marilyn showed no emotion as she spoke. It was simply a fact.

"Oh, I know, sweetheart, your mom told me and I'm so sorry to hear that. That must be so tough for you."

Since when were Dr. Katz and her mom BFFs? Since when was her mom talking about all the personal stuff happening in their house? Wasn't the mom not supposed to get involved in therapy?

Despite the angry thoughts bouncing around Marilyn's head, the understanding in Dr. Katz's eyes—the way she genuinely seemed to feel bad—brought a little blanket of warm comfort to Marilyn's sad, scared heart.

"Yeah," Marilyn said. "It has."

"I know how it feels. My mother died in a car crash a few years ago, and to this day I still can't believe she's gone."

The empathy never left Dr. Katz's eyes once as she talked, and Marilyn realized why. She had gone through the same thing.

Maybe for once, someone actually knew how Marilyn was feeling. It wasn't sympathy—it was empathy. Dr. Katz was speaking from experience.

"I can't believe he's gone either," Marilyn breathed shakily. In the past two-and-a-half months she had never admitted how she felt. She stored everything in a pit inside her stomach, and no one got to go near it—no one got to reach inside.

"Have you talked to anyone about it so far?" Dr. Katz asked.

Marilyn's mouth started to curve into the word "yes," but she hesitated. This was a safe space.

"No. Never."

Dr. Katz showed no signs of surprise as she looked kindly at Marilyn.

"Have you ever wanted to talk about it?"

"Yes."

"What has been the hardest thing for you, since the incident—if you don't mind sharing?"

At this point, Marilyn had dug herself a deep hole, which she was now trapped inside. And since she no longer had the option to go up, her only choice was to dig down deeper.

"The fact that he's never coming back."

The pain in Dr. Katz's eyes revealed that she, too, had faced that same feeling.

"I just want to pretend it's a bad dream," Marilyn surprised herself by saying. "I don't want to face reality."

"I felt the same way with my mother—the hope that it isn't really happening, that it's all a dream, or your imagination."

"Exactly," Marilyn whispered, astonished. Had she really found someone else who shared her emotions, her thoughts? The ones that a few minutes ago she was convinced were abnormal, concerning, weird?

Marilyn's mother never showed any sign of negative emotion—although she was kind and generous, she was reserved and never let anyone see her crack. It left Marilyn feeling alone in her emotions, never quite sure if her mom was feeling the same way.

Shifting in her seat, Dr. Katz said, "These are all completely normal thoughts and feelings. What you and so many others in the world are experiencing is grief."

"I thought I was struggling with depression," Marilyn replied. "That's what my mom said. I thought I was coming here to be properly diagnosed with a depression disorder."

Dr. Katz smiled sadly.

"It can be hard to tell the difference sometimes. Both are completely normal and common but, in general, depression lasts for a while and is not always triggered by a certain event. When you are depressed, your interests, eating habits, and sleeping habits can all change. You could feel like there's no point in anything, in life, and you might sit on the couch for days just feeling sad. Whereas grief is intense sadness caused by a traumatic event, most often death. Unlike depression, grief does not usually qualify as a "disorder" and doesn't usually need medical attention, unless it lasts a very long time and causes thoughts of self-harm. Nothing about your grief is abnormal. It is very common to still feel sad and heartbroken at this stage. The good news is both grief and depression can be helped by talking to a therapist, so you're in the right place."

Relief—warm, friendly, and comforting—sunk into Marilyn's brain and body, soaking her, the way a sponge absorbs water. She was OK. Her deep sorrow and pain was "normal" and "very common." And whatever emotions she was dealing with could be treated and learned to manage.

"You know, I had a female patient around your age, about a year ago," Dr. Katz told Marilyn. "She struggled with very similar grief. Her mother had died in a car crash, and it was a big shock to her whole family. When she came in, she spoke about how she didn't want to let go of her mother, how she couldn't deal with the thought of her being gone forever.

"I asked her what something her mother loved was. Something that reminded her of her mom, something that made her think of her. This girl said that her mom had loved dogs, especially their family dog.

"So she collected a bunch of her dog's loose hairs that he'd shed and the two of us walked over to the river down the street. We stood on top of the bridge and dropped the hairs into the river and watched them fall and float away. It was our way of letting her mom go—watching her float away but still remain on the earth, in the air, in the girl's heart. I don't know if you'd find it beneficial, but my patient really did. Would you maybe want to try doing something like that?"

Marilyn considered the thought for a moment. Did she really want her dad to float away—to leave her forever? That was exactly what she'd been trying to avoid realizing.

"I don't know," Marilyn said skeptically. "I don't think that would help me, because I don't want to think about my dad leaving me."

"I understand that, but I think of it more as 'not really leaving' instead of 'leaving,'" Dr. Katz explained. "I like to think that even though they are not technically with you anymore, you are still together in your memory and your heart, and they are still out there, somewhere."

That was a good point. Maybe it was worth a try.

"OK."

"I don't want to force you to," Dr. Katz said with understanding. "I just think you might find it helpful."

"OK, I'll do it."

Dr. Katz gave Marilyn another twinkling smile.

"I think that's wonderful. We can do that at the end of the month, on the day of our last appointment. but in the meantime, what's something your dad likes? Something that reminds you of him? Maybe you can think about that—"

That wasn't a hard question to answer.

"Roses," Marilyn interrupted immediately. "He loved roses. He said they are a symbol of love and beauty, and he planted them all over our backyard."

"That's so nice—how wonderful! Since your dad liked roses, what if we sprinkle rose petals into the river?" Dr. Katz asked.

"Sure." Marilyn liked that idea. It was beautiful yet meaningful. It represented her dad perfectly.

* * *

THE CHILLY APRIL AIR STUNG MARILYN'S FACE, BUT IN A good way. A thick sheet of snow-white fog engulfed the neighborhood, tormenting everyone with lingering winter weather, while the bright green grass and pink buds forming on the cherry blossoms promised spring was on its way.

As Marilyn and Dr. Katz ambled up the stone bridge, fighting against the intense gusts of winds, the clouds gave way to a small patch of shining sunlight, creating an effect that many would describe as magical.

A slight smile crept up Marilyn's face—the first smile in a long, long time. The day that it had all started—the day she talked to Dr. Katz for the first time, trembling from fear—felt like centuries ago, almost non-existent. She never thought the past month was even possible. How could some doctor have created light in the darkest of times? How could some stranger have helped her make so much progress? How could sitting in a room and expressing how she felt make everything so much clearer? That was still a mystery to Marilyn.

As the two reached the top of the bridge, now high above the rushing gray-blue water, Marilyn clutched her Ziploc bag tight to her chest. She knew it was time, but she still stalled an extra minute, pretending to be very fascinated by a rock that resembled a monkey.

"Are you ready, honey?" Dr. Katz asked Marilyn in her gentle, wouldn't-hurt-a-fly sort of way.

Marilyn scanned the river and then turned to Dr. Katz. "I think so."

She peeled open the plastic bag and extended it out.

"Here, take a handful first."

"Oh, sweetie . . ." Dr. Katz looked touched. "That's nice of you, but this is for you. You're the one letting go."

Marilyn began to draw the bag back, but hesitated.

"Take some. For your mother. It's never too late to let go again."

Dr. Katz seemed to come to the conclusion that Marilyn was going to persist, and if the doctor had learned anything in their therapy lessons, she would know how stubborn the girl was.

"All right, I'll take a few. I appreciate it, dear."

Dr. Katz plunged her hand into the bag and pulled out a small handful of rose petals, each one its own vibrant color.

Marilyn grabbed the rest of the beautiful, dried petals that she had collected from her garden.

"When do we drop them?"

"Whenever you're ready."

"OK." Marilyn took a long, deep breath, soaking in the sun, the air, the sounds of flowing water. "I'll count us down. One . . . Two . . . Three . . . Go!

The two of them released the petals from their hands and watched them slowly flutter down. When they reached the water, they floated gracefully on the surface of the water and slowly made their way down the river.

Marilyn watched closely, not blinking, not moving.

That was her dad.

He was floating away—away from her, away from her family, away from their city. Forever.

He was beautiful, colorful, peaceful. He made everything around him so much better and brighter.

Marilyn would miss him. She already did. She wanted him by her side, holding on to her. She wanted him next to her, physically.

He wasn't gone in her memory, though. In her heart, in the air around her, in the river, he still lingered, and she would hold on to him forever in that way.

She had let him go.

But then again, she hadn't.

What Dreams May Come

Stranded

By Kane Lowell

Creslane Elementary School

"Those guys better be waiting for us," my best friend, Glen, said. He's about four foot eleven inches tall with dark brown hair. He has a good sense of humor and a face covered in freckles.

"Oh, relax," I said. "They're probably still making popcorn." My name is Ted, and I'm ten years old, five foot three inches, and blonde with blue eyes. Everyone was having a sleepover at one of my friend's houses. Glenn and I walked there through a neighborhood after school.

I had suggested the sleepover a few days ago, wanting one last chance to hang out before going on a camping trip for a few weeks. We would be driving, to my disappointment, as I get carsick easily. For the sleepover, we would watch a movie and eat popcorn and candy: a reliable recipe for a great time. The movie we selected was new, and we had been wanting to watch it for a while before it came out.

We approached the house. As soon as I turned the doorknob and cracked open the door, we were greeted by laughter and familiar sights: David sleeping on the couch, Robbie scrolling to find the movie, and Bill popping popcorn while concocting a mixture of junk food. I grinned.

A day later, after the sleepover, we put our bags in the car and my dog Carter got in his kennel. I fed him a treat before we hit the road. The ride started out smoothly but then, a few hours in, something bad happened: we got lost.

A single sign, blocked by a branch, unreadable, was the only thing signaling human civilization. Dad got out to read it, and Mom dropped her phone out the open window. She got out to grab it, leaving me inside.

I decided to stretch my legs and get some fresh air. But when I reached for the door handle, I saw the edge of the narrow road crumble, and was caught by surprise and jerked backwards.

As I was tossed out of my seat, I saw through the window that the car was rolling down the side of a cliff and gaining speed. I hit my ankle and shoulder on the side of the car. A huge branch whacked into it, breaking the door off. I fell out and hit the ground hard. The impact knocked the wind out of me.

The car's tailgate flew open, and Carter, inside his kennel, fell out and landed in the mud. I watched as the car rolled into a river and floated away, getting torn apart in the rapids.

After the last of it disappeared under the raging rapids, I groaned in pain. I sat there for a minute, my shoulder throbbing, but my ankle was my main concern: it was purple, swollen, and as I reached down and touched it gingerly, felt like it was on fire.

I slowly got up and limped over to Carter, who whined and scratched at his cage, which was beaten up and bent. I unlatched it and watched as he got up, and came to me for attention and comfort. When I saw he didn't have any injuries, I breathed a sigh of relief and gave him a scratch behind the ear and a pat on the head.

It was already getting dark, so I decided to find shelter for the night, as I was in no shape to walk. I looked around, surveying the scene. There was a large mountain close by with a big indent about four feet tall and around twenty feet long that faced the river. Perfect. I called for Carter to follow me and headed towards the small cave, limping.

As I approached it, I noticed that it had some small chunks of rock and dirt. The floor looked worn. I wondered if it belonged to an animal. But there were no signs of nearby wildlife, and I couldn't really look for another place to spend the night; I was lucky enough to find one shelter.

When I lay down to go to sleep, though, I found that the floor was much too cold, hard and rocky to try to go to bed on. I endured it for a few minutes, but soon decided to create something to use as a cushion, as the current situation was not working. I could make it out of moss and dead leaves. It would help keep me and Carter to stay warm and shouldn't take too long.

So I told Carter to stay and I went outside. I started pulling lichens off trees and picking up only the driest leaves, which I checked for bugs. I also added handfuls of soft grass and dried those off the best I could on my shirt. I spent a few more minutes collecting, using a pocketknife that I found in my sweatshirt to help.

By then, the moon and the stars were coming out and, through their dim silver light, I saw rain clouds starting to gather. I looked at the bulges of mossy bedding in my pockets and my hand. I decided what I had was enough and started to walk back when I heard howling.

My eyes widened and my heart beat faster as the sound of multiple wolves filled my ears. Despite my ankle, I started running back to the shelter away from what sounded like an eerie song. Based on their howls, they sounded pretty close.

Through the trees, I caught a glimpse of one. It stared at me, and I swear I saw its gaze drop to my limping leg. It knew I was injured. I'd heard before that some animals target wounded prey, but I didn't know about wolves. I didn't really know how dangerous they were, but I didn't intend to find out. I ran faster.

When I reached the shelter, I still didn't relax. I dropped the bedding on the floor, then went down on my knees and, breathing heavily, spread it out on the floor, making an even layer of soft cushion big enough for me and Carter to sleep on. But I didn't feel safe enough to go to sleep, as their howls persisted.

Carter whined and cowered, so I went over and petted him. He seemed to calm down a bit, but it was clear that I wasn't the only one who was worried. I led him over to the bedding and told him to lie down. He listened. Then, I told him to stay, and I went out and lowered myself from the three-foot-tall ledge a couple of feet away from our shelter that led to the river.

There were quite a bit of round rocks that made up the shore. Their sizes ranged from the size of my hand to my head. I grabbed one after another and set it on the small ledge. I didn't pause a second, no matter how loud it was.

Carter came over to me, head slightly tilted, curious what I was doing. After I had a large pile of round stones, I lifted myself back up to the shelter, where I stacked the biggest rocks to form a makeshift wall to help keep the wolves out, if they came. I made it three layers thick, and tall enough to touch the roof. I made it the same way on the other side, then on the edge of the small ledge down to the river. It seemed surprisingly strong and could be removed if you had human hands, but for paws, nothing they did would work. Carter seemed mostly reassured, and so was I. Plus, the wall muted all their howling. So, I told Carter to lie down again, and I lay down with him to help preserve body heat.

Carter drifted off fast, but I was kept from sleeping not just from the invading worry about the coyotes, but also the nagging worry of dying out there. What if I was never found? Even if I survived for a long time, I would become crazy, living far away from anyone else, no contact with anyone again. I steeped in my worry for a while, but it couldn't compete with my tiredness from everything that had happened, and I drifted off to sleep.

It wasn't long before I was jerked awake by the wolves. I sat up and listened, heart pumping. It sounded like they were right outside. They scratched at the rocks, trying to get in. I heard a few howls. By then, Carter was awake. He had his hair raised and was barking loudly. I heard a huge slam, then the sound of rocks tumbling. I didn't know what they were doing, but it wasn't good. They did it twice more, and I backed up to the wall, but Carter stayed slightly ahead of me. He growled at the wolves.

Then, with another crash, one burst through. Carter lunged at it, and they engaged in a snarling battle. He managed to get the wolf pinned, then slashed at its snout. It yelped and escaped from under him, then bolted away.

Carter ran back out with me close behind. He let out an even fiercer growl at the other wolves, but what appeared to be the alpha leapt forward and attacked him. I wanted to do something, but I wasn't sure what I could do. Then I remembered the knife in my pocket. I pulled it out, gathered my courage, and, right as the wolf pined Carter, I threw the knife at it. I couldn't see where it hit, but the wolf yelped loudly and ran off, its pack following.

Breathing heavily, I walked back into the shelter, rebuilt the broken wall, and got back on the makeshift bed. As I sat there in the dark, I wondered what my friends were doing. They were all probably fast asleep in their real beds with a cozy blanket. I shivered. I also wondered what my parents were doing, and if they were searching for me. I decided to get up as early as I could to go back up the hill. With that thought, I closed my eyes and drifted off.

I woke up to the sound of birds chirping outside. I yawned and got up. I had to tell Carter to get up off the bed so I could gather it all up and stuff it in my pockets. I looked around to make sure nothing got left behind, and with that, I removed a few rocks of the wall and headed out, Carter following behind.

The journey up the hill started out good but after a while, my feet got sore and Carter slowed down. I'd been on hikes before, but this was steep, rocky, and hot. Still, I pressed on. After a few hours, I decided to take a rest. I sat down on a rock. Carter started barking and, at first, I couldn't tell what he was barking at, but then I heard the loud whir of a plane. I wasn't sure if it was a search plane but if it wasn't, it would still be another person who could help me. I yelled and waved at it, trying to get its attention, but it passed right by. I called after it until my throat was hoarse, but it kept going until it flew out of sight. I wanted to sit on that rock forever, but I knew I needed to get going. So, I got up and trudged on.

After another hour, I wanted to quit, but then I remembered the plane. It wasn't flying too high, which meant that there was an airport close by. An airport meant I was close to a town. So, I kept going and, after a while, I thought I could see a road through the trees. As I neared it, I saw that I was right. I ran towards it. As soon as I reached it I breathed a sigh of relief. I spotted the same sign from earlier, so I went over to read it. In big white letters, it said WELCOME TO GREEN VALLEY! POPULATION: 1,359. I walked towards it, finally back.

Epilogue

It didn't take much longer after that to get home. Our reunion was emotional, and we were all happy. Apparently, my parents both scoured the forest for me and called the police. They sent someone to look right away, but never found me. They were worried sick the whole time, and they didn't stop worrying until they found me. Carter still has scars from the fight with the wolves. We took him to the vet and he seems fine.

Back home, I realize how much I took for granted. A soft bed, shelter, food, everything. At school, my friends asked me questions about what happened at first, but then things just went back to normal. A few newspaper reporters have asked for the story, but I haven't talked too much about it to them. For now, I'm just glad to be home.

The End

Shipwrecked in the Sky

by Hunter Lowell

Creswell Middle School

The year is 2273.

The New Dawn hurtles through space, moving at the speed of light. Its lightspeed engines have been in development on and off for forty-two years by the private tech company C.E.L.L. They had launched the New Dawn in 2266, seven years earlier. Aboard are fifty adults and twenty-five children in cryosleep, the process in which live beings rest in deep slumber at very low temperatures. This lets bodies stop developing and continue normally once out of sleep.

The New Dawn has left Earth behind, but no one on board feels regretful.

Pollution sent the ozone layer's stability plummeting and temperatures skyrocketing. Most ocean life is extinct, and humanity is in poor health from lack of clean oxygen and nutrients. But the worst of it happened when the last of the ice caps melted and put many major coastal cities underwater. Cities like New York, Tokyo, and Sydney remain uninhabitable. So, C.E.L.L. invited the twenty-five smartest couples with one child each, from all corners of the globe, to escape Earth and start over.

Their destination is a planet seven lightyears away called B-327. The crew calls it Salvator, Latin for Savior. The New Dawn left in secret, leaving humans' only home.

But then, on year six, month eleven, day twenty-three, with one week left in its journey, the New Dawn hits an asteroid field.

I AWAKE, WITH A VIOLENT SHUDDERING IN MY CRYOSLEEP pod. And then the pod flips.

I hear glass shatter and l land on my back. Everything is pitch-dark. I feel the ground rumble under me, and then go still. *What just happened?* I remember my parents and I getting invited by some organization on a spaceship headed to the planet Salvator, trying to start humanity over someplace else. Then we blasted off, were put to sleep in a pod, and somehow, here I am now.

I cough and groan for a minute on my back. I sit up and hit my head on the cushion of my cryosleep pod. The thing is upside down and on top of me. There are glass shards on the floor, but I'm uninjured save for a few scrapes and bruises. All I'm wearing is a skin-tight jumpsuit and the air is cold. I need to take stock of the situation, find my parents, and figure out what happened.

Though the lights are still off, I remember the pods have glass covers and are strapped to the ground. But right now, I need to get out from under this pod. I feel around the top and push upwards with my legs. I feel it give, and I roll out from under it.

There's a loud *clang!* to my right. I stand up and squint around the room, hoping to see anything. I don't remember a light switch anywhere, just that the lights were always on. I'm in the children's bay, where ages one to eighteen are housed. We all should be waking up seven years after liftoff, but no one else is awake as far as I can tell.

All other pods seem intact. I stumble around in the dark, still groggy. My main focus right now is to turn the lights on. I shiver. I also need to get warm. I feel around until I reach a wall. I'm running my hand along it, trying to find a switch when my foot hits a box. I reach inside and I wrap my hand around a cylinder. My thumb slides over a button. *Click.* A circle of fluorescent light beams the wall in front of me. *A flashlight!* I inspect the rest of the box. I find a hammer and a half roll of duct tape as well. I stick the items in my pockets and turn around.

The room has a sealed iron door. I see my overturned cryopod. All the other pods are sound, tethered to the floor. On my pod, I notice one of the straps is unbuckled. That explains how it flipped. But the question is, what was that shaking that caused it?

On the far wall, lockers. I head over to them.

The lockers are all sealed with padlocks, but nothing the hammer can't fix. A few swings and the cheap locks break with ease. After searching each one, I end up with a box cutter razor, a reflective emergency blanket, several hoodies and sweatpants with the C.E.L.L. logo, plus a few pairs of thermal socks and underwear. I pull the thermal wear on, then a pair of pants and a sweatshirt. They all fit me OK, as I was in the kid's room. I also grab a pair of two-way radios from a bag in a locker. They are standard issue for all crew members.

The heavy sliding door won't budge, but there is a maintenance vent in the corner of the room. I pry the grated cover open with the claw of the hammer and lower myself inside. *Right or left?* I decide to come back and try right later. I crawl left and pull up into the captain's cabin. No pods in here. The ship is flown entirely by the onboard artificial intelligence,

Titus. I scan the room, praying to see the robot is intact. And then my flashlight casts over it. Titus.

Titus has a single physical form: a set of treads, a vertical torso, and four spindly arms. Normally, it would automatically do any repairs, probably fixing whatever happened to the ship already, but Titus doesn't look in any condition to be doing maintenance.

The robot is on its side, two arms missing, and a tread gone. But Titus' monitor lights up as I approach.

"Ethan Barrows?" the robotic voice echoes.

"Yes! I thought I was alone!" I yell.

"As I am separate from the main generator, I can still operate. But not physically, I'm afraid," says Titus.

"So, what happened?" I inquire.

"The New Dawn flew through a patch of asteroids. Although the exterior is tough, the interior felt every impact. We're in the clear for now, but not long. We should have a week left until we land in Salvator, but the engines cut off," he explains.

So that's what flipped my pod . . . and Titus, apparently.

"What happened to the power?" I ask.

"When the asteroids made impact with the hull, the whole ship shook. I ran a diagnostic of the ship and learned that the main generator had been ruptured. Now the engines shut off, the heating system is down, and the rest of the asteroids are headed our way."

This sounds horrible. But what terrifies me is the fact that it all rests in my hands. Titus is immobile, which means I need to make all the repairs.

"Can't you just wake everyone up?"

"It would be much too dangerous to open seventy-four cryopods in low temperatures, total darkness, and unresponding engines. I am sorry, Ethan. You will remain on your own,"

"What can I do?"

"You will first need to start up the backup generator on the far side of the ship. Then activate the heating system, or you will die of hypothermia in approximately four hours. Then turn on the engines to steer out of the way of the asteroids. They will make impact in seven hours."

I feel dizzy. The flashlight hits the ground. I drop to my knees, as I realize humanity's last hope for survival rests on my shoulders and time is not on my side.

I set up a radio next to Titus, the talk button held down with tape. I clip the other radio to my collar, collect my supplies and crawl through the vent. Titus guides me through the ship as I explain where I am. No electricity means no security camera feed for him to track me. Plus, every door is sealed, requiring electricity to open. My limbs are icy and I have goosebumps as I make way through the tunnel, heading towards the back of the ship. My head pops up into the bathroom.

Although I had been in every room on the ship before, that was nearly seven years ago. Next, I end up back in the kid's bay, where I take a left in the tunnels into the adults' cryobay. After pulling myself inside, I visit my parents' pods. Like graves. I shake my head. *Can't think like that.*

We're from Australia, and both of my parents have IQ levels over 130. I peer inside. Their resting faces give me hope. I don't bother searching the room for supplies; I'm in a hurry. The tunnel in the corner of the adult's bay is only about ten feet long with one other connecting room: the engine room.

Out of the vent, I look up at a gnarled machine. A hunk of gears, metal, and wires tower above me. The first lightspeed engine. I radio to Titus.

"The engines look fine."

"Good. How is the main generator? Salvageable?"

I peer at a mass of torn metal and showering sparks.

"Completely destroyed," I say.

Thankfully, each of the machines are in different housing units. I shine the flashlight to the right of the generator. An identical but smaller machine seems to be in good shape.

"Found it, Titus,"

"Does it work?"

"One way to find out." I say, switching a lever into its "on" position, then stepping back. Several lights flash and a low humming noise begins. Lights power up overhead. Real ones. I hear the clunk of doors simultaneously opening.

"Yes! Titus! We did it!"

"I see that. Outstanding job, Ethan. But it has dropped to thirty-five degrees on the ship. You need to get the temperature controls back on track, now. You don't have long until hypothermia kills you."

Back in the captain's cabin with Titus, I cut two arm holes in the emergency blanket with the box cutter razor. I then put on thermal socks with custom-cut thumb holes on my hands. I throw on the extra sweatshirts and pants and get ready to leave.

"Temperature is down to twenty-five degrees. Move quickly," Titus tells me. "You work well under pressure. But how well under the cold? You have less than three hours to turn up the temperature."

"I don't need that right now. Let me focus and try not to die. Your facts aren't exactly inspirational," I say.

"Right. But hurry."

I head down from the captain's cabin to the rec room where the temperature panel is located. The rec room is a large, square room with couches, armchairs, tables, and TVs.

Bedrooms were never built because we were supposed to sleep in our cryopods for the duration of the flight.

The panel is held up by two small screws in the wall. During the shaking, though, they have both shaken out. The panel itself hangs out of the wall connected by wires. It should be an easy fix; all I need is a screwdriver. I walk to the adult's bay, hoping to find a toolbox. In the corner, inside a locker (lockers are no obstacle when I have my hammer with me), I find a big zip-up bag full of tools. I grab a small screwdriver and turn around. And then the ship starts shaking.

This time it's like an earthquake. The floor shudders violently and I'm thrown off my feet. The screwdriver flies out of my hand. My head hits the floor and everything goes dark.

Two hours later

"Ethan, wake up. Ethan, wake up. Ethan, wake up. Ethan, wake up."

My eyes flutter open. I'm so cold. "T-T-Titus, I'm here. You c-can stop," I mutter into the radio, teeth chattering.

"Oh, good. Are you fit to walk?" I hear the voice crackle through the radio.

"My head hurts. I'm going back to sleep now."

"Ethan, you are delusional. You have about an hour left before you freeze to death, and you likely have a concussion. Snap out of it and turn that temperature up, or you die."

The robot has my attention now.

"And then everyone else in those pods will die. Your parents, and your friends. You are humankind's last hope. Do you want that?"

"No, I don't."

"Then snap out of it. An asteroid just hit the New Dawn.

It is one of many. The asteroid field is arriving quicker than expected. Now get to the panel."

"Yes, sir."

I feel like I'm getting yelled at, but I know that I need it. I shakily get on my hands and knees. My teeth chatter and I can't feel my fingers as I crawl over to the rec room. I can't imagine trying this without lights or with sealed doors. I sit on my knees at the base of the panel. I lift two hands and clumsily twist the screws into place. My vision is darkening. I'm falling asleep again. I twist the dial until the display reads seventy-three degrees. I let go, drop to my back, and close my eyes.

Titus wakes me up a few hours later.

"Enough rest," he says. "Come see me in the cabin."

I grab a bottle of water and a can of peaches from the emergency food supply. I sit down next to Titus and begin eating. The ship is significantly warmer, and it feels great.

"You have one last step that is crucial to your survival. You need to activate the engines," Titus begins.

"Sounds easy. I was just in the engine room," I say.

"The asteroid field will reach the ship very soon. You need to take a spacewalk and repair a section of thruster that the second asteroid hit. I can guide you."

"Wait, what?"

"And then I can turn on the engines. I can download myself into the ship's control computers and fly the ship away as soon as you are back inside. There are spacesuits for everyone on the Dawn, below the bathroom. There are also repair tools in a closet behind the door to your left."

A spacewalk? I didn't sign up for this.

"OK, Titus. I got this," I say, headed to the supply closet Titus had mentioned.

"The repairs needed are on the left thruster's open-and-close mechanism. If I cannot open the thruster, the propelling force of the flames cannot escape and push the New Dawn forward."

"Uh . . . got it. I think."

I open the supply closet. I grab a welding tool, a welding visor that clips over my helmet, and several scraps of flexible repair metal. In the airlock, I pull on a space suit, clip on my welding visor, and throw my tools in a bag. I go over some safety checks with Titus, then I'm ready. I clip my tether to a hook on the wall. I hit the "open" button and the door slides open, revealing the expanse of space. I throw myself into it.

I have no weight. The New Dawn is equipped with artificial gravity with minimal windows, so I hardly realized until this point that I've really been in space. I grab onto the side of the ship, finding handholds in the metal as I make my way towards the back of the ship.

The thruster appears from behind the New Dawn as I approach the end. I float up to it and sling my bag from over my shoulder. I unzip it and pull out the welding torch. The tool is cordless, designed for space repairs. I inspect the damage. It looks like a meteor has clipped the arm that opens and closes the flap. Half the arm is connected to the ship, the other half to the flap, but there is no connection between the two.

Luckily, the arm snapped on a long stretch of cylinder, and not a moving joint. I flex the repair metal around the snapped arm and start melting metal to metal. I continue this for a few minutes until I'm satisfied.

"Titus, get ready to fly, I'm on my way back," I say through the helmet's communications radio.

"Move quickly. The asteroids are nearly here," Titus' voice booms.

I scramble towards the airlock. It is about thirty feet away, when something flashes in the corner of my eye. I look up to see an asteroid headed right towards me, along with around fifty others. A rock hits me in the side before I have time to react. I lose all grip on the wall and get thrown into space. The New Dawn gets smaller and smaller as I float away. I frantically try to pull myself in with the tether, until it goes taut. Asteroids fly everywhere as I pull myself back towards the ship. For a moment, I believe that I will run out of energy before I reach the ship. My arms burn and my fingers cramp.

Now the New Dawn is in arm's reach. I haul myself into the airlock. I hit the button on the wall and the door closes. I lay on my back and radio to Titus.

"You're clear! Go!"

The ship instantly shoots away. I hang onto the door handle as we peel away.

Titus stops the ship so I can gather more food and water, then sit in the cabin with him. I lean my head back, sigh, and get ready for the remaining ride.

One year later

The New Dawn landed safely one week later. My parents wouldn't have believed what happened if not for Titus backing up my story!

Anyway, Salvator is absolutely beautiful. We've set up a town and begun work on cities for future generations. We continue to make breakthroughs every day. Salvator is a fresh start, a chance for us to prove that we can learn from our mistakes and keep our new home clean.

ORBIT

BY JT MYERS

Elmira High School

"Do it."
"But sir—"
"I said do it. We do not back down to threats. We will
make a show of our power and establish this nation as
a force to be reckoned with."
"Sir, if we fire, everyone will. The world—"
"You know better than to question your superiors.
Now push the damn button."

—The beginning of the end of the world

A steel tube sat on the fringe of a gravitational pull around a miniscule blue and green marble floating in a black ocean of emptiness.

Effortlessly gliding at 18,000 miles per hour, the tube made no sound. It split the vacuum like a knife, but there was no air for a scream. Sunlight bathed the black wings of the gliding lump of steel and fed it—just enough—to keep life inside.

Beneath it, the spinning, glittering marble was infested with fleas squabbling amongst themselves over imaginary values and digital affection. They told themselves that if they had more of each (and more of everything), then their specific little flea mattered. Their little flea was loved above all. Their little flea had purpose.

Outside of those little fleas, nothing else mattered. Not the deaths of stars nor the explosive births of galaxies. Not the glittering comets streaking by nor the universe's mesmerizing expansion. Not even the imminent threat of doom looming over them.

And the little satellite that floated far above was left forgotten.

The radio clicked on inside and static poured out of the speaker. The spaceman twisted a red dial no larger than a coat button and homed in on the signal beamed up from Earth.

Fragmented voices became audible, coming together like a child playing with a jigsaw, forcing each piece together until they find the one that fits. The sentences formed slowly until a steady stream of fuzzy words filled the metal walls.

"Can you hear me? Hello? This is ground control. Come in . . ." Static interrupted the name, but the satellite pilot knew the transmission was for him.

"Yeah, I can hear you loud and clear. What is it?"

The radio continued, still interrupted by patchy static.

"Listen, things are getting pretty tense down here. The president . . . a direct order to bring everyone back in ASAP. They think the safest thing for all . . . to return them back to the ground."

"You're getting ahead of yourself there, buddy. What's going on?"

"If anything happens, they think your chances are bett . . . munications could get knocked out, then we'd have no way of reaching you for a long time—too long of a time! You would be completely stranded. We . . . ur best return path—" the machine rambled out and echoed slightly off the cold steel chamber.

"Hey!" the astronaut interjected. "You still haven't told me what's going on! What is happening down there?"

"Things are heating up . . . just invaded . . . world war is looking likely. They want . . . back just in . . . calculated flightpath sending . . ."

"Hey! Hey, are you there? I'm losing your signal."

The pilot frantically twisted the red dial to home back in on the messenger from Earth.

"Are you there?" he exclaimed.

Only static answered.

There was no more signal being broadcast. The spaceman assumed that communications were impacted as the messenger had said was possible. He was now utterly alone and doomed to a steel coffin.

Without any way to contact the ground, there was no way to plan a safe way back. Within the next three months, he would completely run out of the stores of food and water onboard. He was a dead man walking or, rather, floating, in his peculiar instance. And he knew it.

He flipped the switch, and a sharp click abruptly silenced the static in the room. The stillness in the air flooded his ears and brain. His thoughts didn't have the space to process in his head because his skull was compressing, squeezing the mind it was supposed to protect.

The panic was overwhelming. The spaceman dropped to the floor and put his hands in his hair and grasped, just to give him anything to feel besides the metal around him. His hands released and slid down to his ears in an attempt to block out the deafening silence.

Curled into a ball on the floor, he blacked out.

Hours later, a yellow light flashed on a screen on the far wall. It beeped and the spaceman was startled awake.

Calmer, he got up and clicked the button beneath the screen. A map showing a calculated course of entry into the Earth's orbit appeared. The message was transmitted just in time before the signal was cut off.

The astronaut stepped away. He slowly breathed, relaxing himself.

With renewed vigor, the spaceman moved to the front of the craft and started booting up controls for an altered course. The details sent in the message showed a narrow window that provided for reentry into the atmosphere. Anything outside of that time frame, the spacecraft would not have the force nor fuel to push through and would instead skip right off the top of the atmosphere, with deadly repercussions.

There was just one problem. The course that was sent was incomplete. The signal was, in fact, cut off before the message was fully sent. It was missing the commands for the spacecraft's autopilot system. The astronaut would have to steer the course himself using the course provided.

He knew he was capable and very well-trained for situations like this. But knowing how to do something and following through are two entirely different worlds. He would have to be perfect if he ever wanted to make it back. The spaceman took a moment to absorb this realization, to accept it, and to move on. He needed to get back home, and he wasn't going to let his own nerves hold him back.

He stretched his arms in front of him with his fingers entwined and popped his knuckles. The spaceman shook out the nervous feeling that crawled up his spine and he took command of the controls to his little shuttle. He flipped switches and twisted knobs. The craft awoke like a dragon, quaking and roaring, a flame set ablaze in its belly. Colors flickered across the panels and screens. Charts and indicators and flight instruments became visible as the screens warmed up.

Grasping the helm of the ship with one hand, the pilot upped the throttle with the other. Boosters on the sides and rear of the satellite breathed and propelled it forward and towards Earth. Screens showed every slight change in the satellite's path.

The astronaut paid close attention to the changes on the screens glowing in front of him and to the calculated course he was transmitted. He made adjustments, ever so slightly, to keep a flawless trajectory forward. Any miscue or twitch of the hand would be disastrous, taking away the needed angle to pierce the protective outer layers of the atmosphere.

Keeping steady, the satellite built up momentum, hurtling like a bug on a freeway towards a windshield. It reached the entry point, right on cue, and began to break through the outermost atmosphere. The front of the spacecraft began to heat up, flames erupting around the front as it pushed inwards.

Suddenly, outside of the satellite, far in front of it, a thunderous sound erupted: *BOOOOM!* A great force rocked the whole shuttle.

The hull screamed and shook violently. The spaceman panicked, thinking he must have made a mistake. The screens in front of him had shown he was still on course leading up to this point, but now he was sent careening backwards and back outside of Earth's protective bubble.

The spaceman scrambled around the controls, attempting to stabilize the shuttle and bring it to a stop. When it was back under control, he checked his course and the ship's condition. He had flown without flaw, but something had happened, ruining his chances of making it back home.

Home. He went to the window on the side of the hull to look upon Earth, his home, but he could only look in horror.

Dark clouds in the shapes of mushrooms grew across the continents, hundreds of them, across the visible side of the planet. Fire whipped around the edges of each cloud and, in between the mushrooms, were fading fireflies, little flashes of light glittering across the ground.

"My God," was all the man uttered.

He noticed one mushroom towering far into the sky, higher than all the other mushroom clouds and even the pure natural clouds. It left a deep wound in the planet, spreading for what must have been a thousand miles in the webbed shape of cracked glass. The mushroom extended toward the direction the ship was headed through the atmosphere. The force of that blast must have been what expelled him from his course, launching him back into orbit around the planet.

While the spaceman was captivated by the continued assault across the planet, a new light appeared on one of the screens. "CARBON-OXYGEN RECYCLER DAMAGED" spanned the screen in bolded red letters.

"Oh, no. No no no no no," the astronaut rattled off.

The most important function of the ship to a passenger was now gone, damaged in the failed return to Earth. As if the destruction of his planet wasn't enough, he was now sentenced to his own doom, long before the months' worth of provisions would ever run out. Without the recycler, only three hours of breathable air remained.

"NO!" he finally screamed and punched the screen that displayed the honest but cold and terrifying message. It cracked like the Earth's crust below and the words faded out.

The hand that pulled away dripped blood. The space-man, fully aware of his fate and knowing there were no more chances for optimism, lashed out in his metal coffin. He picked up a coffee mug from his morning breakfast and slung it across the room. He screamed and jumped and smashed the walls with his hands and any object he could grab.

How is one supposed to react when the world has ended, and they are next?

Eventually, the astronaut expressed the last of his rage and collapsed to the floor once more. He looked out the window above him and saw the decimated and burning planet. Tears streamed down his face as he cried for all the people he knew back on Earth; he cried for all the people he didn't.

The last man alive could no longer bring himself to observe the tragedy of his world, so he found a new window to peer through.

Through this new one, he found a pretty scene of glitter across the black. The stars twinkled and shimmered, distracting him from everything. He peered beyond, and knew that, somewhere else, on some other planet, there was life. This thought comforted him enough, to know that Earth was not taking the random, amazing miracle it had with it to its grave.

The spaceman whispered to the void, to bring a peaceful thought to himself as the oxygen expired.

"I wish you luck. I know you can do better than us."

Whispers in the Woods

by Lauren Ellison

Marist High School

When the bell rang announcing the start of lunch, Willow pushed out of her woodshop seat, waving goodbye to Mr. Hamley. He was a round man, with bald spots on the back of his head. Willow wondered if he didn't know he had them, or if he felt the absence of hair when he anxiously stroked the back of his head during lessons.

She passed the gym on her way outside, getting a look at the basketball freaks, sweaty and yelling at their teammates. Stepping outside, Willow felt the harsh bite of the winter wind pushing her brown hair into her face, but was thankful for the breeze anyway. She had become sweaty during woodshop class, working on her memorial box for her brother, Aaron.

Aaron was sixteen, just three years older than Willow when he was killed. Murdered, by a cop. Now, two years later, fifteen-year-old Willow was terrified of cops.

She was such a wimp, ducking behind a bush when a police car passed, keeping her head down walking by one on the street. The only thing that helped drown these thoughts was walking. Willow walked everywhere, to school, to the library, to the store. During lunch, which was now, Willow walked to the track field, crossed it, and hopped the fence that kept the students safe from danger. Or was supposed to, anyway. Behind the fence was lush Oregon forest, vibrantly green compared to the sad beige of the school.

Willow traveled deeper into the woods, led by nothing but her feet and an empty head. The trees shrouded the pale sun's light, and she became cold in her hoodie and jeans. As Willow walked, she checked her watch. Twenty minutes left of peace and solitude.

Still looking down, something caught her attention just to the side of her, something shiny. Willow turned and walked towards it, her curiosity too loud to ignore. What she found was an old and rusty pull saw, like the ones they used in wood-shop. Willow wouldn't call herself a collector, per se, but she did like keeping things she found. Into her backpack it went.

Willow's mom was already there when she arrived home from school at 3:45, her eyes glued to the news on the TV. This meant another night shift, the third in a row this week.

"Hey, sweetie," her mom said without looking at her.

"Hi, Mom. What time are you leaving tonight?" Willow asked, shutting the door behind her.

Ignoring her daughter's question, her mom asked, frowning, "Do you know these kids? They go to your school. They've been missing for over forty-eight hours, poor things."

Willow looked at the screen and saw Leo with his curly brown hair, and Priya, her beautiful smile and green glasses on display.

"Yeah, they're in my woodshop class this year. Maybe they ran away together," she joked.

As Willow walked up the stairs to her room, her mom called, "Willow, sweetie, I love you. Be safe walking outside, OK?"

"I will, Mom. I love you too," Willow replied.

She couldn't bear the defeated look on her mom's face.

Willow knew she was thinking about Aaron, who she hadn't talked about in what seemed like forever. Willow wished they talked about him more. She missed him so much.

Willow woke up groggy and dazed from another night of restless sleep. Getting ready for school, she brushed her teeth, put on clothes, and set out a banana for her mom, who should be getting back from work at the hospital soon. The fifteen-minute walk to school seemed quicker than normal, probably because Willow couldn't wait to finish her box in woodshop. Once she arrived to class, she got to work right away, finding the tools she needed to finalize her memorial box. Staring at the wall of tools for what felt like hours, Willow couldn't find the draw knife. Mr. Hamley smiled at her as she made her way over to his desk.

"Good morning, Willow. How's your box coming along?"

She smiled back, saying, "It's going good, but I can't find the draw knife. I wanted to use it to round out the edges. Do you know where it is?"

"Nope. Went missing about a day ago. I haven't a clue where it went. Sorry, Willow."

Mr. Hamley almost looked nervous when he said this, which confused Willow. It wasn't necessarily his fault, some kid could have stolen it or something, which he couldn't help. Whatever. She'd have to work with what she had.

That night, Willow had the strangest dream. She was walking in the woods behind school, hand in hand with Aaron. He led her to a big, knotted tree, where a draw knife lay at the base of its trunk. Just then, there was a rustling behind them, and they turned around to see a hooded figure running past them, a pair of familiar glasses in hand.

"Hey! Where are you going? What are you running from?" Willow yelled.

The figure ignored her and ran on. The back of their jacket was unnerving. A white skull was surrounded by flies, with sharp weapons bordering it.

Aaron turned towards her, a frantic look on his face. Before, he had been smiling and serene, but now he was shaking his head at Willow, mouthing the words, "This tree," and, "Be careful."

Willow woke up sweaty and afraid, and she couldn't go back to sleep. She turned on her lamp and grabbed the pull saw from underneath her bed, inspecting it. It was worn down, the wooden handle chipped and scarred. The blade was still sharp, though. Really sharp, actually, like it had just been sharpened.

There was a red stain at the base of the handle, and Willow held it closer to her lamp. It looked a lot like blood. Willow was pretty sure it was blood. She stuffed it back underneath her bed and read a book to try and muffle the thoughts swarming her head.

"What was this saw used for? Why was it in the woods behind the school? Why did I keep it?"

While getting ready for school the next morning, Willow decided that she was going to find the knotted tree that Aaron took her to last night. Who knew, maybe the missing draw knife from woodshop would be lying in front of it, like in her dream. Or maybe the tree was just a figment of her imagination.

The day dragged on until woodshop, when she noticed a familiar leather jacket that Stephan was wearing. The back depicted a decaying skull surrounded by flies. Exactly like the hooded figure in her dream. Did he have something to do with the missing students? What about Mr. Hamley's missing tools? Willow couldn't help but wonder about the situation.

      Winners Anthology

Willow walked for fifteen minutes until she found the knotted tree. The draw knife was exactly where Aaron led her in her dream, and beside it lay a broken pair of green glasses. Willow's heart pounded as she recalled her classmates' faces on the TV screen.

She carefully picked up Priya's glasses, horrified. This was evidence in an investigation, a police investigation. Willow knew she shouldn't have, but she stuffed the glasses in her pocket and stashed the knife into her backpack, in an endless loop of asking, "Why would Stephan want Priya and Leo dead? Where did he take them?"

Willow needed melatonin that night. After her dream the night before, and the day she'd had, she didn't hesitate to reach for the bottle. She fell asleep quickly.

Willow woke up in the woods, walking with Aaron again. Except this time there were screams in the distance, and Aaron's face was coated in blood. Her own hands were coated in blood. It was then that she noticed she was holding the pull saw that she had found days ago, which was now sticky with blood. Leo's curly brown hair was stuck to it, wrapped around the blade like a Christmas ribbon. Aaron was crying beside her, silent tears streaming down his face.

"Aaron, talk to me," Willow pleaded. "Is Stephan the one who killed them? Please, just say something!"

"Wake up now, Willow, go to the knotted tree."

Aaron stared deeply into her eyes as he said this, and it felt like real life, like this was actually happening.

Willow didn't notice until the tear ran down her cheek that she was crying, scared and sad.

"I'm scared, I don't want to go to the woods by myself."

Aaron held her shoulders tightly, urging, "You need to go now! Wake up!"

At once Willow was awake and out of bed, putting on her coat and sliding into her slippers like a robot. Her alarm clock showed that it was two in the morning. Willow knew that her mom would be gone for at least three more hours, so she shut and locked the door behind her, exposing herself to the cold air outside.

Willow ran as fast as she could to the school, cutting through neighbors' yards and jumping over bushes. She hopped the fence and realized that she hadn't brought anything, a flashlight, a weapon, anything to help her with her task, but she decided that it was too late to turn back. She didn't even know what her task was, just that her dead brother was telling her to find that tree.

Willow rushed into the woods, blindly hopping over tree limbs and rocks, dodging everything blocking her path. She didn't know how she knew where the tree was, but she knew she was getting close. In the distance, Willow heard a sound, and she slowed down to a walking pace.

Up ahead, she caught a glimpse of light coming from a flashlight. She leaned up against the knotted tree's trunk and slowly looked around it, to where the light was coming from. There she saw two figures, one larger and standing over the other, the latter kneeling, bent over themself, their blonde hair cascading over their face.

Willow's heart felt like it was beating out of her chest, she was so frightened. She knew that blonde hair. It was Priya, crying, while the hidden figure yelled at her. Willow watched the scene play out, careful not to make a sound. The larger figure was hooded, holding a knife to Priya's throat. Suddenly, Priya lurched forward and pushed the hood off her captor, revealing their identity.

Willow saw who it was and gasped so loudly that both Priya and her captor looked in her direction.

Willow turned and ran back home so fast, hopping the fence and winding through lawns, looking back to see if the man was chasing after her. Once she was inside, she locked the door behind her and peeked through the curtained windows.

Questions were flying around her mind like a blizzard.

"What am I going to do? How can I stop this without going to the police? Should I not have left Priya with him? Why am I such a wimp? What does Mr. Hamley want from them?"

Willow didn't go back to sleep. She couldn't, not with the events that had just occurred replaying in her brain. When her mom pulled up in the driveway at five, Willow ran upstairs into her room and pretended to be asleep. She felt empty as she got ready for school and said goodbye to her mom.

Willow walked slowly to school, not wanting to go to woodshop. Mr. Hamley would be there, and she knew what he had done. It wasn't Stephan, like she had thought, but actually her teacher, the nice, welcoming balding man. Willow was still in shock as she walked into his classroom and slid quietly into her seat, careful not to make eye contact with anyone.

The class went by slowly, and Willow kept her head down the whole time, faking a headache. She was terrified of the reality she was in; she was a witness to a kidnapping, and she was harboring evidence from the crime. Willow knew what she had to do, but she just couldn't face it. The police had killed her brother, she couldn't go to them. What if they didn't believe her, or they thought she was the one who killed Leo and Priya, if they were dead? Mr. Hamley might be saving them for something bigger; Willow didn't want to imagine the plans he had.

The bell rang, and instead of going to her next class, Willow walked home. She snuck past her mom, sleeping soundly in her room, and went to her own. Willow slept.

In her dream, Willow was in Aaron's room with him, playing Monopoly. It was his turn, so he grabbed the spinner and spun, quietly hoping under his breath for a three. Willow looked at the board, seeing where his token was and where three moves would get him. Her heart sank, and tears stung her eyes.

"No, Aaron. I can't go to the police. You of all people should understand, they killed you!"

Willow scooted back on the carpet, farther from the game. The spinner was still spinning, perfectly centered between three and four.

Aaron looked at her with sad eyes, saying gently, "It's OK. You know you need to do this." A tear fell down his cheek and he closed his eyes. "Keeping this a secret won't bring me back, it will just result in more death."

Willow was sobbing now, hugging her knees to her chest.

"I just miss you so much, you don't understand."

Aaron appeared by her side, taking his sister into his arms and holding her head to his shoulder.

"I miss you too, Wilsy. Go to the police station. You're brave and smart and too young to hold this inside of you. I love you forever."

There was a clink on the board, and Aaron and Willow both crawled to the game. The spinner had stopped, right on three. Willow wasn't about to cheat; she would do as the board ordered. She was going to jail.

"I'd like to report a crime. Please." Willow' voice cracked on the word "crime." The whole walk to the police station, Willow had been repeating that sentence perfectly. Of course, she messed up when it really mattered. The door shut behind her, and she stood in the lobby awkwardly, feeling in her pockets for Priya's glasses. She felt the weight of the saw and knife in her backpack. A nice-looking woman came up to her slowly, like she was a scared animal.

"OK, sweetie. Come with me." The woman gestured to a long hallway behind her, and Willow followed.

She cried, but she did it. Willow told the police everything, her body shaking with anxiety and sadness for her classmates. The officer thanked her as he bagged the evidence, told her she was free to go for now, and that they would start searching as soon as they were done here.

Before heading home, Willow walked around town to clear her mind. She was scared that Mr. Hamley would know she told the police. She was scared they would want her to go to court. She was scared of the future, in general.

When Willow got home, her mom was hunched on the couch, watching the news intently. A picture of Mr. Hamley was displayed, along with the heading, "Missing Children Found in High School Teacher's Shed." Willow sat beside her mom to listen to the reporter.

"After police received a tip and evidence from a citizen of the community, officers found freshman Priya Lang and Leo Matthews in the shed of their teacher, Mike Hamley's backyard. Hamley has not yet been questioned. The two students are back home, safe with their families. The police and families of the recovered students thank this anonymous source for helping to find them."

Willow leaned back on the couch, disbelieving of the events that had occurred. Her classmates were alive because of her, because she went to the police. She looked at her mom, noticing the dark circles under her eyes and her messy hair. Willow leaned closer and hugged her mom, saying, "I love you."

"Oh sweetie, I love you too. I'm so glad your friends are safe, and that your teacher is gone. It's just unbelievable, that could've been you!"

"It wasn't."

"Well, it could've been. I can't lose you. You know that, right?"

Her mom searched for an answer in Willow eyes, which were now brimming with tears. She couldn't imagine how hard it must have been for her mom, losing a son when he hadn't lived a full life like she had envisioned.

"Can we talk about him? Aaron? I miss him so much," Willow asked.

Her mom's eyes sparkled with tears.

"Of course. We should have, a long time ago. I'm so sorry." She paused, then laughed, smiling, "Remember his dance he would do when he was scared?"

Willow hugged her mom tighter, letting the tears flow.

She laughed and said, "Yeah, it was so weird. Like a kangaroo. I can't believe I was the spider-killer in the house, and not him."

They held each other until the tears stopped, until they were too tired to talk. Mom and daughter fell asleep on the couch, embracing each other.

River of Dreams

Zonglou

by Leo Kuhl

Charlemagne French Immersion
Elementary School

"Toss me the rope," Creeker called.

He dared not look down. He'd come so far, but now he could fall; it could all end. Creeker would not let that happen, not if he had anything to do about it. However, in this case, he may not have anything to do except hope.

In the distance he heard a trumpet sound as the semi-furnoms came running towards the cliff.

"Please," Creeker panted. "Help."

It seemed like Milio had run off with the rope in hand. Trusting him was probably a mistake, but looking back on what he'd done, Creeker decided that he'd made a lot of mistakes.

Creeker heard another trumpet sound followed by the sound of the thumping feet of the semifurnoms running across the ground. Creeker was too curious to just stay staring pressed against the wall of the cliff, so he made the mistake of looking down.

Thousands of semifurnoms came with swords, grappling hooks, and torches, running to the cliff in a fit of rage. Their leader, Valgrot, had a dagger that he carried in his right hand.

Semifurnoms were ugly creatures. Covered in scales like lizards, they stood on two feet and walked like humans. Their faces were covered with warts, and their scales often shed. Unlike furnoms, semifurnoms did not have wings, but they had fangs that were often covered in blood after a meal. They had three-toed feet with claws on each toe.

Creeker felt himself shake with fear, which made it even harder to balance on the slim ledge he was standing on. All of a sudden, he felt a big shake in the cliff as the semifurnoms threw their grappling hooks onto the cliff.

Creeker started to fall, down to the semifurnoms, to his death.

Creeker fell around eighty feet before his shirt got caught on a grappling hook. That didn't stop him from falling though; it only slowed his fall down. However, it slowed it just enough for Creeker to be able to grasp part of the grappling hook.

He caught himself twenty feet above the ground, but then a semifurnom started climbing the grappling hook that Creeker was hanging on to. Creeker jumped down from the grappling hook and landed on the ground with a thud.

He felt like he might have broken some bones. In fact, he'd definitely broken some bones—but none of that mattered to him because he had survived. There was no other time he'd felt so happy to be alive. Probably because he'd never fallen off a cliff before.

However, his joy quickly ended when he realized that he was circled by semifurnoms who now looked extremely hungry. He sprinted—well, he limp-sprinted, but it was as fast as he could go. He started running but only made it forty feet before he saw that right in front of him was Valgrot.

* * *

"Wait, so if you don't want to eat me, what do you want with me?" Creeker asked.

He was sitting down tied to a tree in the middle of the semifurnoms' camp smelling Valgrot's horrid stench.

"Information," Valgrot responded in his raspy voice. "Let me start out by asking you, what are you doing here?"

Creeker explained, "Well, the king is always looking for more power, and in this case more power means more land. So, he asked Milio and me to go exploring in this area. I always liked exploring, and it's my dream to get the Best Explorer medal. We were going to meet up with a much bigger group of people in the Southern Rock Mountains, then head west from there, but as you can see, things didn't turn out so well for me."

"Ahhh, so you decided to trespass on our land, which was a grave mistake," Valgrot growled.

"Yeah, I'm kinda starting to realize that now," Creeker said.

"You stupid humans have always held a grudge against us semifurnoms for absolutely no reason," Valgrot said, shifting his position on his throne.

"Well, I mean, to be fair, you guys do always seem like you're trying to kill us," Creeker pointed out. "But anyway, it was fun chatting and—"

"This conversation isn't over yet. I have one more question for you," Valgrot said in a particularly raspy voice.

"OK, what's that?" Creeker asked.

Valgrot smiled.

"What do you know of Zonglou?"

"You mean the cursed Island?" Creeker asked.

Valgrot smiled again. "Ahh, so you've heard of it."

"Well yeah, but it's cursed so it's not a great place for a vacation," Creeker said.

"You know how to get there, don't you?" Valgrot's smile showed a lot more teeth than Creeker thought he had.

"What makes you think that?" Creeker asked.

"I can tell." Valgrot's display of teeth really made Creeker think that, at any second, he would be semifurnom food.

Unfortunately, Valgrot was right, Creeker did know where it was, and Creeker had a feeling there was no point in saying he didn't.

Valgrot continued, "How do you get there?"

"I don't really feel any inclination whatsoever to tell you that," Creeker stated.

Anger flashed through Valgrot's eyes.

"This isn't the friendly chit chat you think it is."

He pointed a dagger at Creeker's throat.

Creeker swallowed hard.

"OK then."

He handed Valgrot a map of the country.

"There, you see that cliff just south of us? Go there, then go southwest, and you'll make it to Zonglou."

Valgrot smiled.

"Guards, you may free this prisoner. Make haste for Zonglou!"

Two guards escorted Creeker outside of the large camp that smelled of smoke from the fire, then they released him and followed the rest of the semifurnoms in a brisk march south.

A few moments later, Creeker could no longer hear the thumping of their feet and was left alone in the wilderness. The sun was high in the sky and there was plenty of time before dusk, but Creeker knew that in order to not be caught in the wilderness at night he had to start moving.

He was very curious about what Valgrot wanted with Zonglou, so he decided to follow the semifurnoms. However, he knew that if he headed west, he could travel through the valley between the Southern Rock Mountains and the Western Rock Mountains and avoid going uphill. Then he would stop at the big city of Snowville, which, despite its name, didn't get much snow. In Snowville he could gather a crew to go southwest to Zonglou, and they could maybe get there before the semifurnoms.

Creeker was afraid of what Valgrot wanted with Zonglou. He felt like there was something that Valgrot knew about it that he didn't, and it seemed extremely important to Valgrot. That could only mean something bad for Creeker.

Creeker shivered as a cool breeze swept through the forest he was standing in. Even though it was a very sunny day, the dense forest shaded Creeker making it quite a bit cooler than his spot on the cliff.

There was something strange about the forest. There always seemed to be a breeze that swept through the trees but nowhere else around it. There was also always a thin layer of mist that gathered at the level of Creeker's ankles. But what sent a chill down Creeker's bones was the name of the river that went through the forest: The Death River.

Few dared ask how The Death River got its name, and Creeker wasn't really wanting to find out right then, either.

Creeker began to walk at a brisk pace towards the valley. He knew that there were only fields of grass and no strange forests in between the valley and Snowville, so he was eager to get past the valley.

In about half an hour, Creeker arrived at the valley. On either side of it there were tall mountains with snow at their peaks. The valley was only five hundred feet wide, and The Death River took up a lot of that.

Creeker was careful to remain close to the base of the Southern Rock Mountains so he wouldn't get too near the river.

About three hours had passed, and it was getting late in the day. Creeker predicted it was around four-thirty. The sun would set at six-thirty, so he still had two more hours left to make it to Snowville and be safe during the night.

He was beginning to see the end of the valley in sight when he heard the unmistakable sound of thumping feet.

"Oh, no," he thought. "How did the semifurnoms get here?"

He looked up, and Valgrot was around two hundred feet higher than he was standing on a rock facing out towards the west away from Creeker. Then he left his spot and Creeker heard the thumping of their feet heading away into the distance.

Creeker was pretty sure that the semifurnoms were headed down a trail that wound down the mountain on the west side, and he was pretty sure it would take them an hour. That meant two things. One was that he was safe on the northern side of the mountain, and two, was that if he was in the meadows in an hour when the semifurnoms made it down the mountain, they would see him and then they would know what he was doing.

Creeker knew he had to quicken his pace in order to make it to Snowville in time, so he began to run.

Twenty minutes later he was out of the valley and running through the yellowish green grass of the fields leading up to Snowville.

He glanced behind him and was relieved to see that there were no semifurnoms running at him with torches.

Since he was tired, he slowed to a walk and continued on to Snowville, now a thirty-minute walk away.

He was only one hundred yards away from the first of many houses in the city of Snowville when he looked behind him again. This time he saw the first semifurnom come out of the trees with a torch in its hand.

The semifurnom hadn't seen Creeker yet, so Creeker dove down into the tall grass. His heart pounded against his chest. The furnoms were fast runners, so if they saw him, they would run at him with torches and follow him into the city, which would mean not only that he would be semifurnom food but the whole city would be semifurnom food.

The semifurnoms would normally be reluctant to go into the city of Snowville because the king lived there, and he and the semifurnoms had long ago made an agreement that they would each stay on their land. However, since Creeker had trespassed on their land, they might not care about agreements they made if it meant a lot of food.

Creeker slowly inched forward on his stomach, keeping low so the semifurnoms wouldn't see him. He continued inching forward all the way up to the city, where he got up and hid among a small crowd of people. In the distance he saw the whole group of semifurnoms running southwest.

Creeker went to the downtown area of Snowville and, with his money, bought a room at the Snowville Hotel for the night.

Snowville was the biggest and most interesting city in the country. Unlike most big cities, Snowville didn't really have any outskirts. It just went from fields of grass to a hustling bustling town. However, the city was also large in terms of square footage, all very busy.

Creeker ate dinner at a nice cafe in the downtown area, and then he went into the hotel. When he arrived, there was a group of people sitting, talking, and singing around the fire.

It was, in fact, the search party he was supposed to meet up with at the South Rock Mountains!

Creeker walked up to a man playing the guitar.

"Excuse me," he said.

The man turned around toward him.

"Hi, have you come to sing?"

"Uh, no. Look, this may seem a bit straightforward, but Valgrot and his group of semifurnoms are heading to Zonglou, the cursed Island, and I need to get there first to investigate it. And I was wondering if you could take me there with your group?" Creeker asked.

"Zonglou eh? Well, I don't know . . ." the man trailed off.

"Listen to Creeker."

Creeker turned around to see Milio standing right behind him.

"Hi, Creeker," he smiled. "Sorry, I got lost earlier."

Creeker was confused. Why was Milio being so nice to him? And what did he mean that he got lost? But he had bigger things to worry about. He turned back towards the man.

"I suppose. But in exchange I would expect some money," the man said.

"I'll deal with that," Milio said. "Creeker, you should get a good night's sleep."

Since Creeker was tired he didn't argue and walked upstairs to his room.

* * *

"I'll stay here and watch over the horses while you guys go explore Zonglou. Sound good?" Milio repeated for the fourth time.

"All right, I think we all know the plan now," said Douglas, the man Creeker saw playing the guitar the previous night.

It was early in the morning and Creeker had successfully made it to Zonglou, just as planned. The semifurnoms were nowhere in sight, and Creeker was excited to find out what it was the semifurnoms were after. He was also nervous though, because Zonglou was a cursed island after all.

"Hop on in," Douglas said to Creeker, gesturing to the little boat.

Creeker hopped in, and then Douglas rowed them and the rest of the crew, except Milio, to the shore of Zonglou, which was only about a hundred feet away from the mainland.

When they arrived, Creeker got out first and the rest followed him. He stepped into the forest and started walking towards the big volcano in the center of the island.

The island wasn't very big at all. Just a volcano, a lava lake, and a tiny forest. However, it was called a cursed island for a reason. It was so misty that Creeker couldn't see more than two feet in any direction, which meant he couldn't see the ground. That made it very difficult to avoid the lava lake. However, Creeker didn't really think it was bad enough to be called a cursed island.

"Careful!" Douglas shouted.

Creeker paused mid step.

"Do you feel how hot it is here?" Douglas continued, "The lava lake must be right here so be careful to walk around it."

Creeker walked around the lake using the heat as a guide.

A few minutes later someone shouted, "Come over here!"

Creeker hurried over to where they were, carefully not stepping in the lava lake.

"Look in that cave! There is a shiny piece of metal; it's a treasure chest poking out! Hand me a shovel, Douglas, and I can dig it out!" the man exclaimed.

Creeker stepped forward and bent down so he could see the ground and, sure enough, jutting out from the dirt was the corner of a treasure chest. Douglas tossed the man a shovel, and he started digging.

Creeker was amazed looking at the treasure chest; he had never seen one before! But then there was a rumble as the volcano started to erupt. Huge boulders went crashing to the ground.

"We have to get off Zonglou!" Creeker shouted.

"But what about the treasure?" the man asked.

Then, the pieces all clicked together in Creeker's head.

"No, leave it, and get out of the cave immediately."

The man hesitated, then reluctantly stopped digging, and everyone walked out of the cave. Right after they did, a big boulder came crashing in front of the cave entrance blocking it entirely. If they hadn't listened to Creeker, they would have been trapped.

"The semifurnoms didn't want to get a treasure from Zonglou! They wanted me to think there was something important on Zonglou and to attempt to get it but die in the process," Creeker said, mostly to himself.

Creeker led the others to the shore, ready to get in the boats and go to the mainland, but instead the boats had been smashed by a boulder, and angry semifurnoms lined the shore. Creeker caught a glimpse of Milio taking gold from the semifurnoms and riding away on a horse.

Of course! Milio had been the one who convinced Douglas to go to Zonglou because he was working with the semifurnoms and knew they would die. Creeker was so angry; he had thought that Milio was being nicer, but really, he was only being worse.

Creeker turned to Douglas.

"I have a plan," he said.

CREEKER WAS SITTING IN A TREE ON THE MAINLAND. HE had managed an epic escape from Zonglou. The whole crew, except Milio, swam to the shore without taking a breath in between, because if they did the semifurnoms, would know they were coming. Then they snuck up on the semifurnoms and caused a diversion while Douglas escaped to go get the king for help. Creeker smiled; it was a brilliant plan.

"You can't stay up there forever," Valgrot growled for the hundredth time.

Creeker had climbed the tree so the semifurnoms would stay where they were waiting at the bottom because semifurnoms are terrible tree climbers. Just then, Douglas came riding on a horse alongside the king and the king's soldiers.

They fought the semifurnoms and easily won, and the semifurnoms were locked up along with Milio, who was found riding his horse with sacks of gold.

The following day, the king placed the Best Explorer medal upon Creeker! Creeker had dreamed about this day!

He also gave Creeker lots of money for doing such a good job catching the semifurnoms. Creeker returned to Snowville with Douglas and the crew, and when he drifted off to sleep, he felt better than ever.

The Green Ember

by Kai Suzumura

Ridgeline Montessori Public Charter School

Chapter One

Dalen sat in the foyer of his home, an old lodge deep in the forests a few miles outside of Bantell, a small hamlet. The lodge was passed down to him by his father when he died, and since then, Dalen called it home.

He rested in an armchair, reading a report on the recent battle of Leupuith, over at the eastern border of Krefta, the country he lived in. The sound of the midday birds was sweet and crisp to his ears, and he paused reading to listen.

Slowly though, another sound came into his consciousness: the gallop of a horse. Dalen straightened in his chair and looked down the path that led to the lodge, waiting to see the source of the noise. An armored rider for the Order of The Ivory Gauntlet (OTIG) came into view, riding quickly toward him and making no attempt to slow down. Dalen furrowed his brow and stood up.

"That's close enough!" he yelled, and closed his hand around a spiked club hidden behind a wooden post.

"Message from the OTIG headquarters!" the rider called, and Dalen relaxed, setting the club down.

The horseman pulled on his reins and the horse slid to a

stop. The rider then proceeded to pull a parchment roll from a bag hanging on the saddle, and handed it to Dalen. After that, they took off once more, speeding back down the path and disappearing into the forest.

Dalen took the message and sat back down. He opened the wax seal and read the letter. OTIG was calling for him again, saying it was urgent.

Order of The Ivory Gauntlet often carried out work that was too dangerous or time consuming for the Kreftan government's armed forces to do. They were like an all-terrain special forces. The OTIG soldiers were a direct branch of the Rangers, working as an armored soldiers force with them, instead of as the normal Ranger, who used their skills of archery, stealth, and poison-making to safely take down large groups of enemies alone. Dalen had expected to take a break from fighting, having just come back from fighting in the war of Leupuith as an OTIG commander. He had thought he would be free of duty for a while, but maybe not.

* * *

As summer turned to fall, the nights got progressively colder, tamping down the already dwindling spirits of the small party of OTIG soldiers camped among the sparse pines and towering oaks of the flaming forest. The name came from the way that the forest lit up with sunlight every morning, giving an illusion that the trees were in flames.

They had been out in the wilds and mostly far from civilization for many weeks. It was the infamous band of Korzak Raiders that led them to sleep in the cold. These raiders were orcish beastmen who lived in separate groups, though they all were united, in the caves and caverns of soaring mountains.

Travelers and caravans would occasionally report being attacked and robbed of their goods by these bands late at night. But recently, these groups of orcs had gotten out of hand, boldly attacking villages and farming communities that dwelled near the mountains of Kurndmure Marsh, killing livestock and destroying crops. The Order of The Ivory Gauntlet soldiers were here to hunt them down, in accord with the Rangers, to assist them in their tasks of protecting the country and its citizens.

The cold had arrived with a loud gust of wind just before dawn. It chilled the camp sentries through their thick coats, helping to keep them awake. Unfortunately for the soldiers, something else had arrived with the icy wind, and it gathered now, just inside the shadows of the tree line.

OTIG scout Mathew huddled by the trunk of a pine, trying to gain more warmth from his heavy fur coat than it offered him. His mind wandered to breakfast, he was eager to fill his belly and warm up after the long hours standing guard. He thought of all the previous campaigns he had taken part in with the Order of The Ivory Gauntlet, all across Krefta. Mathew wondered when he would be able to go home, for the first time in over a year, after being deployed in Colften, Krefta's neighboring country.

But as he thought that, out of the corner of his eye, he saw a flash of movement. Just after he saw the movement, the sentry near him scrambled to their feet and grabbed a spear, but in the process of doing so, they were thrown violently backwards, landing with a cry.

Mathew grabbed the scabbard next to him and unsheathed the blade within. He rushed to the soldier, checking to see what had happened to him. There was a crossbow bolt deep in his side that was seeping blood onto the frozen and cracked ground. Mathew looked into the darkness, but saw nothing, just the silent trees. Mathew opened his mouth to sound the alarm and wake the soldiers.

"Medic, I need a medic!" Mathew cried, as he fumbled to stop the bleeding. A minute later, a surgeon rubbing their eyes rushed to their assistance, opening a leather satchel slung over their shoulder.

"I've got him," he said, then thrust a needle into their side, just above the wound. The needle was full of a mixture that numbed the body so that a medic could treat a soldier's wound without it hurting so much that they moved around, making it hard to work. The wounded soldier flinched, but then relaxed. The medic pulled out of the satchel a handful of small, green, and soft needle-like leaves, all attached to a stringy vine. The medic thrust them into the wound, and then quickly wrapped the soldier's midsection with a thick white cloth.

"The plant will stop the bleeding for the time being," the medic explained, as he closed his satchel, then said, "Can you stand up?"

"I think so," the soldier said, coming carefully to his feet with the help of the medic. Then, they walked slowly back to the tent.

* * *

It had been about an hour since the encounter with the unknown archer, and the group was breaking camp.

"Where are we going next, sir?" asked one of the soldiers, an older veteran of war with a grimy face and a tangled beard.

"Glaze, an old mining town not far from here, is where the orcs plan to go next."

"They plan to take a rare gem called the Green Ember that was found in the mines there just a few days ago and give it to the leader of their greater organization," Commander Dalen said.

"Then we better hurry up!" said the soldier.

"That's the spirit! All right soldiers, on the double, we are leaving in an hour!"

Chapter Two

The OTIG group left shortly after the attack, heading for a town named Glaze, which was the Krozak's target.

Glaze was a mining town that sat on a rocky bluff overlooking the miles of dead trees and swampy, foggy fields dubbed Kurndmure Marsh. The town was encased with tall wooden walls and iron gates that protected the ore and gems mined within.

When they arrived, they hustled everyone inside of their homes, since they did not know when the orcs were coming, and they did not want any of the civilians to get injured.

In the center of this town, a large bell tower reached up to the clouds, and surveyed the surrounding country. Behind it were the homes of the residents, and the town eating house. In front of the tower, there was the front gate and the village green, where the animals of farmers could be brought to be fed and get exercise.

It was under the tower that the group waited, but as they did so, they piled crates and barrels in multiple locations by the town's front gate to provide a place for the soldiers to hide. They also set up a watch to warn the soldiers when the raiders were coming, at the top of the tower.

* * *

Mathew sat at the top of Glaze's bell tower, which allowed him to see the surrounding countryside easily. He was the guard that Dalen had posted, to warn the soldiers of the raiders' approach.

Mathew had not been up there long before he heard it. The sound was somewhat like distant thunder that got louder and louder, going from being inaudible to well-noticeable. The sound was carried through the wind, reaching Mathew's ears before the soldiers'.

Then he saw the source of the sound. A quarter mile away down the road were the orcs, identifiable by the armor they wore. They were on horseback, and quickly approaching. Mathew jumped up from the old worn chair that he had been sitting in and leaned over the railing of the bell tower and yelled down to his commander.

"Sir, a group of orcs, about eight of them, approaching fast!"

Mathew did not wait for an answer, and swung around, grabbed his weapon, a long-range crossbow made of polished mahogany. From a quiver leaning on the balcony railing, he drew a long bolt, almost as long as a longbow arrow, and loaded it into the crossbow's firing chamber; he then moved over to the railing and hid his body behind the thick post supporting the tower roof.

Meanwhile Dalen and his soldiers were readying weapons and concealing themselves. Now they, too, could hear the horses, and clutched their weapons tightly in anticipation.

Then, suddenly, the raiders appeared in the frame of the town's gate, in a ragged formation that was more of a blob than ranks of any sort. Seeing no people, they stopped and looked around, confused.

The lead orc awkwardly sheathed his blade and called out to the deserted streets: "My dear town of Glaze, we seek food, and lodging . . . Is anyone here?"

Suddenly, there was a loud crack, and the raiders looked up at the bell tower, where the sound had come from. Unfortunately for Mathew, the fact that the leader turned his head saved him, as a bit of the helmet now blocked his previously exposed neck. Mathew's bolt slammed into that bit of helmet, deflecting off it. Although he was still alive, the leader was thrown off his horse, landing with a thud. Then, taking that opportunity, the OTIG soldiers charged.

Dalen jumped up from the crate he was crouched behind and charged. He did not yell as he attempted to stay hidden as long as possible. As he neared a raider, they turned and shouted in alarm, drawing their sword, but were too slow. Dalen bashed them in the side of the head with the edge of his shield, then slid his sword between the bottom of the orc's cuirass and their belt, then up into their vitals, killing them instantly. He was glad to find that his soldiers had also charged, taking the raiders completely by surprise.

By this time, the orc leader had recovered from his fall and was advancing slowly on Dalen. The OTIG commander withdrew his sword from the lifeless body and turned to face the lead raider. The leader swung at Dalen's right shoulder, shouting an insult at him. Dalen countered him by again bringing the edge of his shield to the inside of the raider's arm. Now, since his left arm was across his body, he completed the motion by turning and smashing his armored elbow into the lead raider's sternum. The raider doubled over, and dropped his sword, so Dalen used that opportunity by bringing his armored knee into their face, wincing at the crunch made by the impact.

At this point, half the raiders had been either killed or badly injured and two of the OTIG soldiers were badly injured with only one who had passed on. The raiders, find-ing their leader and a lot of their own soldiers dead, backed away from the battle and retreated to the forest.

The Krozac raiders put up the illusion of retreating with fear, but Dalen sensed something else. While trying to decipher his uncertainty, Dalen caught the eye of one of the orcs, who quickly looked away to the houses, then back at him, then slipped away into the trees. Dalen turned to look at where the raider had looked and saw movement down an alleyway. The movement was not of his soldiers, but of orcs on horseback slipping through the town's back gate.

"I am so stupid, I never put a guard at the rear of the town," he said to himself, then called to his soldiers.

"We got raiders at the back gate, let's get them."

Then he ran off down the alley. At the back gate there was no sign of the raiders, just the distant sound of horses running away from the town. Dalen cursed, sheathing his sword, and walked back to his soldiers.

"All right, the raiders got the artifact—that is my fault, as I was too careless—and are headed off to someplace probably halfway across Krefta, and we have no way to know where they went," Dalen said to his soldiers who were gathered in a half circle in front of him.

"We could try to track them," one of the soldiers suggested.

But Dalen shook his head, "I really do not think so. We are soldiers and I have no doubt that they hid their tracks."

"Man, if only the Rangers were working on this with us instead of working alone, we would probably have caught up to them by now," one of the soldiers said, and the other soldiers muttered agreements.

"Those Rangers are so good at tracking that they can practically track flying birds," another soldier said.

"Hold it, first of all, we technically are Rangers and, second, I could track them if you like. I hunt a lot in the forests around where I live, and I would say I am pretty good at it," a soldier said.

One of his friends replied to him, "You would say."

"We should let him try, anything that will help us catch those bandits is welcomed," Dalen said.

When no one else had anything to say, he continued, "Right then, let's get going, we shouldn't waste daylight."

Chapter Three

The OTIG soldiers left the town of Glaze, following the trail of the raiders high into the mountains east of Kurndmure Marsh, where the air was frigid and quickly blew away their morale. They had been traveling for two days and were tired of continuing the way that they were currently. Only, around lunch of that second day, they tracked the raiders to a cave, set deep in a crevasse of the mountain, dark and forbidding.

Upon entering the cave, they found a series of dim, but quite well-maintained living spaces that consisted of multiple large rooms. Each room had roughly polished floors and walls that were furnished with animal skin rugs, tapestries, and cushioned chairs. Passing through the rooms, they found no bandits, just half-open dressers and cabinets, along with strewn clothing—the sign of hasty packing.

"It looks as if they took their things and left," Dalen said, shaking his head angrily.

"No, my guess is that they heard us coming, but for some reason are heading further into the cave. All their tracks are leading that way," the tracker responded.

"But . . . how?" Dalen said, confused.

"Well, we were riding like the king's cavalry, and rode right up to the entrance. Also, there was that person who shot a sentry a few days ago, my guess was that they were an orc," the tracker said.

"Come on, let's follow them."

So, the group followed the tracks down a dark tunnel only lit by the tracker's torch and glowing mushrooms that lined the walls. Eventually it opened into a more spacious tunnel that, in some places, was filled with large pools of water, and they continued for a while longer.

"What if the Rangers already found the bandits, and we are doing this for nothing?" a soldier asked.

"The Rangers never came through here. Last I heard they were on the other side of these mountains asking around for clues," the tracker said. They continued in silence, that was only broken by a soldier slipping and cursing.

"And here we are, the end of the path, no sign of it continuing," the tracker said, but then suddenly cried out as an arrow hit his arm.

The soldiers rushed forward and formed a shield wall, protecting them from arrows. Then another group of soldiers in a shield wall came up behind them, and the group in front continued on, locating where the arrow had been shot from and advancing to that position. Then two other groups continued up behind them, going to the left and right.

They found orcs behind piles of rocks, firing at them, and they quickly took them down, but were then encountered by orcs behind shields who fought them with axes. After a few minutes, the battle was over and the orcs, along with their commander, were captured.

"Well, we got the silly gem, and made it out without too many casualties. I would say that is a win," said the tracker to the group, who agreed.

But then he was cut off by a new voice. Crouching in the shadows were about four Rangers, and they had their bows readied.

"Stop right there, you are under arrest for thievery, orcs!" the rangers said.

The OTIG soldiers looked at each other, then started laughing at the misunderstanding. It would be a long explanation.

The Rose Theater

by Ishika Chakraborty

South Eugene High School

There were four courtyards in the Novani Palace, one for each wing. In the beginning, there had been talk of establishing a fifth at the heart of the royal residence, only to be discouraged at the queen's request. She claimed to want a greenhouse instead for roses, which was an odd request, considering how she had never even taken clippings for the vases in the east and west wings, let alone planted a single seed in her life.

In the end, the greenhouse was never built, to no one's surprise. In its place, an open-air theater had been erected, suitable for the warm climate of Novanon and the people's penchant for astrology. The seats were upholstered in rich red velvet, and the foundations built from the finest mahogany. A singular balcony gilded in gold looked out upon the rest of the theater, intended for the royal family's viewing pleasure. As a last addition, a retractable glass dome was fashioned for the unlikely event of rain.

Ahren found the theater lovelier than any other room in the palace. Its simplicity was one not found elsewhere, and prying eyes seldom wandered over hundreds of rows of seats in search of the princess.

It was such a shame, then, to have part of her adoration stripped away by the installation of gaudily embellished curtains to frame the stage. No one would ever dare say so, for fear of having their heads chopped off, but it was downright filthy the way the royal family spent money on the most unnecessary of indulgences.

She heard the whispers, every now and then. Talk of revolutions, of impassioned rage amongst the peasants and middle-class. She felt the sharp eyes of every palace servant every time she walked the halls, like pinpricks of acid rain. Her parents might say otherwise, but Ahren was not stupid; she knew half of them were spies, she knew of the botched assassination plans. She knew that it was only a matter of time before she became the target.

She was no stranger to the bitterness and resentment Novanis regarded her with when she was in the presence of her parents, when their attention had been diverted by something frivolous or when their practiced disregard for the betterment of the kingdom felt like a slap in the face. She wasn't quite sure what they expected her to do about it. Perhaps nothing at all. Perhaps they only liked the idea of having someone to blame, a scapegoat for their troubles.

Someone more assertive might have taken the chance and used it to their advantage. But she could not be their savior, for she was too afraid and complacent to do much more than stand with knees locked and eyes pried open, a step back and to the left of her parents, doomed to an eternity on the sidelines in fear of being noticed.

Now, on the first day of the Viridian Festival, sitting alone in the balcony of the theater, she wondered again at the unfairness of it all. Neglectful monarchs and a society on the brink of collapse.

Bloodshed was inevitable. It hovered on the horizon much like the palace held its breath when the king was in one of his moods. Ahren's hands felt clammy. The stars had begun to show through the open roof, winking down at her. She imagined what they might say if they could speak; would they tell her of peaceful kingdoms and empires beyond the border? Would they murmur secrets of the revolution in her ear, lead her to the most hopeful future for Novanon? Or, if they were cowards, would they warn her of her father's rage and her mother's greed for confrontation hot at his heels?

What Novanon had yet to realize was that Ahren liked the king and queen about as much as they did, and often even less on bad days. On bad days, huddled under a mound of the most obscenely embroidered blankets, she trembled with rage, teeth gritted, hands clenched so tight her nails bit at the soft skin of her palms. On bad days, she thought of every bruise, every cut, and wondered what it might be like to rid her people of their horrible rulers once and for all.

She never did anything. Ahren had never been one for action. She was too afraid, too complacent. It was why she could never be the proper martyr Novanon deserved, the face of their rebellion. The bone-deep ache of abandonment and the shadows of physical torment had rendered her a husk of a human, a shell made to hold broken dreams and a statue-like apathy.

She watched the curtains begin to rise. The rest of the theater was empty, devoid of a single soul other than hers. Something about it all seemed wrong, bizarre. The air stood still, eerily silent. Was the first day of the Viridian Festival not cause for celebration? Where were the familiar smells and sounds of joyous hope?

The curtains framed the stage like heavy clouds. Below, illuminated by blinding stage lights, stood two figures. Their postures were awkward, heavy and unsure, like someone had taken control of their limbs and made them stand before a ghost audience.

A shaky exhale, and then another. Each breath misted in the air. Bizarre. It was the middle of summer.

The lights adjusted enough for Ahren to recognize the figures. She did not gasp, did not shout. She remained the phantom spectator she had been born to be. A two-man show was nothing to be surprised about.

Their faces contorted in desperation. She thought they must have seen her, if the horrified anguish in her mother's eyes was any indication. Ahren said nothing, hands folded neatly in her lap. The empty theater felt larger than any room ever had.

Above it all she sat, like a deity forced to watch its creations tear themselves apart. They moved like marionettes in sharp, aborted movements, each line a plea for help, each laugh a shriek of pain. Whatever—whoever—controlled them showed no mercy, and the pure adrenaline of fear steered them through each act and scene of the play.

It might have been unbearable to watch if it were anyone else. Ahren's fingers felt cold but she kept them where they were, unable to look away from the gleaming stage and its unwilling stars. When they bowed, she could not clap. How could she? It had been perhaps the most awful rendition of the play she had ever seen.

She made herself stand. Would they call out to her, beg for her aid? What could she even say? *Yes*, for she feared the sting of her father's hand? *Yes*, for she dreaded the cut of her mother's needles against her arms?

They said nothing. They did not even move, faces frozen in agony.

There was a ringing in Ahren's ears.

✳ ✳ ✳

T HE SECOND DAY OF THE V IRIDIAN F ESTIVAL WAS OFTEN characterized by the sharing of sweets. Ahren had hoped to be woken by the honey smell of delicate pastries from the kitchens. Instead, she found herself once more in the theater.

She couldn't remember what had happened after the performance the night before. She must have retired to her rooms, petrified at the idea of her parents stepping off the stage in her direction, hoping for it to have been a dream, a horrible dream she might forget.

The theater looked the same as before. Empty, colder than it should have been, open to the heavens. Rose and gold streaked above her like thick layers of paint on a portraitist's canvas.

Something told her tonight would be no different.

They appeared on the stage, clad in the garish costumes characteristic of court entertainers, faces no less horrifically confused than before. Ahren found herself unable to remember if she had seen her parents this morning. Had there even been a morning? Had she dreamt it all, the puppet-like show?

She watched the whole thing from beginning to end, tracked the way the king's sweeping gestures began to slow, eyed the way the queen's words became more strained. They were not used to performing. They were not used to being anything other than spoiled and cruel. They were not used to being on the receiving end of fear. They were not used to anything other than glee and extravagant pleasures.

They bowed just as night fell. Another dream? Perhaps the last blow to the head had been her last. Perhaps this was only a coma, or a sick form of purgatory before she would meet her end.

She stood and clapped.

* * *

Ahren thought she understood now.

She had heard stories from the witches and court sorcerers. They spoke in hushed tones of strange happenings in other kingdoms, in places of political unrest or tragic circumstances. Circuits of time, where the proper chronology of reality became corrupted and forced to repeat, over and over, until something changed.

Ahren thought this might be one of those doomed loops. Was it a punishment for her? For her parents? For them all, their indifference, and her passivity?

They moved sluggishly tonight, less fear on their faces and more resignation, their muscles weary from having done the same performance twice already. It was interesting, in a way, how the day would reset but not their bodies.

To change things up, Ahren did not clap this time. Instead waved her handkerchief, the universal sign for an encore.

* * *

Five more nights passed in succession. After each one, the royal couple seemed more exhausted than ever before. Would it ever end? Ahren had begun to tire of it all, but she would never say so; it would not do to insult fate.

On the eighth night of the Viridian Festival—for she had begun to count them as nights of the festival even if time existed in a vacuum—the performance went past nightfall.

In the past, they bowed as soon as the sky darkened. Now, with weak legs and bags beneath their eyes, they seemed not to have the energy to perform at the rate they had begun.

It was pitiful.

* * *

THE NINTH NIGHT, HER MOTHER'S NOSE BEGAN TO BLEED halfway through a soliloquy. Ahren was ashamed to admit it gave her a sick sense of satisfaction.

* * *

WAS IT HER FAULT?

* * *

THE TENTH NIGHT, IT WAS CLEAR THEY WERE NEARING their end. Never had she seen two people look so much like desiccated corpses, yet still be able to move and speak.

There were tears trailing down her father's face at the end of the first act. A smile spread unbidden across Ahren's face.

By the end of the performance, she thought they might collapse. Still, they bowed, and she clapped.

* * *

TRADITIONALLY, THE ELEVENTH NIGHT WAS THE LAST NIGHT of the Viridian Festival. Ahren had a suspicion it would also be the last night of the time loop, the last performance. Would her parents be given a second chance at saving their kingdom, or would they take their last breaths on the stage?

"You know the answer," the stars hissed to her.

And she did. For hadn't she wished for this? Hadn't she hoped for retribution, for revenge? Hadn't she, in the deepest, darkest parts of her core, wished for their death in the most painfully artistic way? They did not deserve mercy. They deserved everything they had been given.

She saw the light dim in their eyes before the sun had set. Awash in the glow of dusk, the two bodies lay upon the stage, under dimmed stage lights and a warm breeze, for the cold chill of the theater had dissipated.

Realm of Forgotten Dreams   123

This was what she had wanted. The loop had never been a product of their actions, but one of her desires.

She thought there might have been blood surrounding the corpses. It was hard to tell from so high up. She felt more powerful than ever before.

The stars were the only witnesses to her laughter.